WE WERE PROMISED SPOTLIGHTS

WE WERE PROMISED SPOTLIGHTS

Lindsay Sproul

putnam

G. P. PUTNAM'S SONS

G. P. PUTNAM'S SONS
An imprint of Penguin Random House LLC, New York

Visit us online at penguinrandomhouse.com

LIBRARY OF CONGRESS CATALOGING-IN-PUBLICATION DATA
Names: Sproul, Lindsay, author.
Title: We were promised spotlights / Lindsay Sproul.
Description: New York: G. P. Putnam's Sons, [2020] | Summary: "When small-town
homecoming queen Taylor Garland comes out as gay, she embarks
on a journey of painful self-discovery and challenges the closed-minded
thinking of those around her"—Provided by publisher.
Identifiers: LCCN 2019009144 (print) | LCCN 2019011559 (ebook) |
ISBN 9781524738549 (ebook) | ISBN 9781524738532 (hardcover)
Subjects: | CYAC: Lesbians—Fiction. | Coming out (Sexual orientation)—Fiction. |
Coming of age—Fiction.
Classification: LCC PZ7.1.S7178 (ebook) | LCC PZ7.1.S7178 We 2020 (print) |
DDC [Fic]—dc23
LC record available at https://lccn.loc.gov/2019009144

Printed in the United States of America
ISBN 9781524738532

1 3 5 7 9 10 8 6 4 2

Design by Kristie Radwilowicz
Text set in Electra LT Std

This book is dedicated to

the Marshfield High School

class of 2003 — stay cute and cool!

Scars are souvenirs you never lose
The past is never far
Did you lose yourself somewhere out there
Did you get to be a star

—Goo Goo Dolls, "Name"

Hopuonk, Massachusetts, 1999

The Secret Bathroom

I went into the bathroom outside the gymnasium, which was all decorated like "An Evening in Paris," because I knew I was going to throw up.

It was the secret bathroom, the single-stall one tucked behind the staircase, where you went if you didn't want to be seen or heard. When I got inside, Corvis McClellan was there, smoking a cigarette.

I hated Corvis McClellan.

I mean, I was supposed to hate her. Only I was starting to miss her now that it was senior year and everyone was getting ready for graduation. She used to be one of us. Every day at recess, we played four square—Susan Blackford, Heather Flynn, Corvis, and me—but that ended in seventh grade.

Corvis gave me a pitying look.

"That homecoming crown looks stupid on you," she said.

I gripped the side of the sink, trying not to do this in front of her. Corvis wasn't a person I wanted to throw up in front of.

The crown was floppy and made of the same cardboard as the Burger King ones, only it was spray-painted gold and had a tiny

Eiffel Tower on the side, which was pushing my ear down. She was right. I looked like a dildo.

"What are you even doing here?" I asked her.

Corvis should have been insecure, but she wasn't. She had jaundiced-looking skin, lips that were too small, and hair that was always greasy.

My date, Brad O'Halloran, was just voted homecoming king. I let him go down on me a month before in the back of his Datsun, and a few days later, my vagina felt like it was full of fire ants.

I ran into Corvis in the waiting room of the gynecologist's office next to the plasma donation center in the strip mall by the highway. I was sitting there with a pamphlet in my lap that said GENITAL HERPES AND YOU.

She looked up from her book and gave me a tight smile. "Nice going," she said, and I wanted to murder her.

"Are you going to barf?" she asked me now. My crown was slipping off.

She put her hand on my back and moved it in slow circles. We hadn't touched since seventh grade, just after she passed me the note I used to destroy her.

I could have held it down before that, but her touch made me feel green. There it was, my dinner, regurgitated in hot chunks in the sink.

When I was done, we sat on the cool tile of the floor.

"Why are you being nice to me?" I asked her, wiping sweat off my forehead with the back of my hand.

She shrugged.

"I don't know," she said. "You look like shit."

The real problem with Corvis was that she knew. She knew I dated Brad because the other girls wanted him, and I wanted the other girls.

I wanted my best friend, Susan, to hug me for a really, really, really long time while I buried my face in her stomach and Melissa Etheridge played in the background. I wanted her to drive me to California, and then I wanted to die in her hair.

"Want a cigarette?" Corvis asked.

"I want . . . a scar." A big, terrible-looking one that would make people afraid of me but not feel sorry for me.

So far, no matter what was going on in the world, no matter which unpronounceable countries were at war, Corvis had always been there, wearing her backpack covered in patches.

But not for much longer. Corvis got good grades, and even though she wasn't pretty, she had that rare glow of a special person, or at least a person who believes she's special.

She looked like someone who'd just set her house on fire. She looked like someone who was going to ride away on a horse and never come back.

I imagined her leaving, spending nights in a long chain of different states, in stale motel rooms where headlight beams crawled across the walls, and she would have girlfriends, and she would not be ashamed.

After she left, I would be stuck with all the assholes who loved pretending that the gymnasium really *was* Paris, who thought I was lucky for being pretty. Maybe I would start to believe them after a while.

I looked like a homecoming queen. Probably someday, I would be a dental hygienist.

"You'll be okay," she said.

I didn't believe her.

There was such a private peace in her eyes. I couldn't know how she got to where she was now. I could only see that she was there.

The Cliff

Taylor Garland. The other kids said it all the time, my name. I was like a brand. My mother was too—Sandra Garland, the queen of Hopuonk. She didn't let me call her Mom, so we were on a first-name basis.

"Taylor!" someone shouted—a girl's voice. Maybe Heather? PJ? Or one of the wannabes, like Bridget Murphy or Jessica O'Grady?

I sat in the parking lot, rubbing my temples. I didn't want anyone to see me with Corvis in the bathroom, so I took off. The music from the dance still beat in my chest. I was pretty sure my underwear was showing.

"Taylor!" A guy this time, then more joined in. They followed me around, their collective voices like a giant mouth. Always hungry, always wanting, always asking.

Even though the dance was still supposed to be in full swing, a sudden crowd had formed around me, sweating, needy, and helpless in their sequined dresses and rented tuxes, now reeking of vodka. I tucked my dress between my legs and looked up at them.

Every small town needs a star. Our football team was total crap, and nobody outside of New England cared about lacrosse or girls' field hockey. So I was the star, just like Sandra had been.

In Hopuonk, Massachusetts, the star is the queen. I used to think queens were rulers, but now I see that they are figureheads.

"Are you okay?" Brad asked, reaching for my shoulder. He stood tall and clean-looking, his biceps visible through his tux, his hair combed like a Ken doll's. I dodged his hand.

"Are you drunk enough?" asked Heather, captain of the cheerleading squad and expert at backflips and punch fronts, pulling a flask out of her clutch. She leaned against someone's rusty car, her red sequined dress cut so low that it came dangerously close to showing her nipples.

"Are you going to Scottie's after-party?" asked PJ Greenberg. She was our school's drama star, and she followed me around constantly. Even though she was talented, drama wasn't exactly considered cool. Pink lipstick was smeared on her teeth.

Susan stared at me, waiting. Her floor-length tube-top dress hugged her hips, and her eyelashes made me want to cry. She shivered, and I thought that no one so perfect should ever be cold. I reached for her hand, and she pulled me up.

Scottie Mahoney's after-party was the last place I wanted to go. I wanted to do something different for once.

I should be running through a field, I thought. *I should be gambling away my work money. I should be hitchhiking to California. I should be doing anything but this.*

"No," I said. I adjusted my crown, which promptly drooped again. "I have the best bad idea."

They stared at me, waiting.

"Fuck Scottie's party," I said. "We're jumping off Fourth Cliff."

Bridge and cliff jumping were big in Hopuonk, just like bonfires on the beach and drinking in the woods on the fire trails. Fourth Cliff was the highest, the most dangerous—the cliff none of us had jumped from yet. It was the cliff someone's drunk uncle had supposedly died jumping from after a school dance in the 1960s. I pictured the dead uncle, glowing like a white stone in the sand at night, his denim jacket that looked slept-in, his cleft chin, his expression tinged with rage and wisdom.

They all stared in disbelief. I realized that for me, it was a game, to see how far they'd follow me.

I didn't want to go home. I wanted to create a story with a big enough climax for it to end with me sleeping in Susan's bed. Something risky enough that I could ditch Brad.

Standing in the parking lot, with everyone staring at me, I thought, *Maybe I'll die jumping off Fourth Cliff, and maybe it will feel amazing, like turning into glitter and then disappearing forever.*

"Come *on!*" I said.

Everyone started piling into cars, tulle spilling out of closed doors.

Susan clung to me as we walked to her car, her tight dress hugging her ass and clinging to her legs. Dark tendrils of hair slipped loose from her bun and curled in the salty air, defying her hair spray. Me, Susan, and Heather drove to the dance together in Susan's car at my request. After we took photos at the pre-party, I wanted to escape from Brad, though I pretended it was because we needed girl time.

I checked for Brad and spotted him far behind us, watching me but still climbing into Jake Finnegan's pickup.

I scanned the parking lot again, checking for Corvis.

"I don't think we should do this," Susan whispered. "Are you sure we should do this?"

There was Corvis, pressed against her passenger-side door, making out with Kristen Duffy, the tuba player. Kristen's hand cupped the back of Corvis's neck, and Corvis had her arms around Kristen's back, where the cheap black lace of her dress bunched around her love handles. My stomach burned.

"One hundred percent," I whispered back to Susan. "You'll love it. You'll shit a million stars."

Cool girls whisper. I learned this in first grade. Also, cool girls drink vodka until they're sick and someone has to take them home. On Mondays, cool girls whisper about who drove them home, and how they were too drunk to remember anything.

Because we were still in high school, we were allowed to cling to each other. But I knew this would end, because Sandra never clung to anyone.

Sandra still whispered, though. That's how the mystery of who my father was stayed alive, like the breath of a sleeping cat. The suspicion of truth in my story—despite the near impossibility of this truth—was one of the reasons I suspected I stayed popular.

Another reason was that I crushed people, like I crushed Corvis in seventh grade. She no longer seemed crushed, though, which both infuriated me and made me want her back. I either wanted to be her, be near her, or crush her again.

I took shotgun in Susan's car without paying attention to who else was there, since I knew none of them were Brad.

"Look at Corvis McClellan," Heather said from the back seat. "That's a wicked disgusting display."

I put my hand on Susan's thigh as we watched Hopuonk go by out the window: The maple trees and the winding roads full of sand and broken oyster shells. The slanted colonial houses that needed paint jobs, and the rusted-out cars that sat in driveways up on cinder blocks, waiting to be fixed.

"So gross," I said.

In her attempt to drive while drunk, Susan ran a stop sign, then pressed the brake afterward. That seemed like a metaphor for my life.

Heather shuddered, opened her dainty little flask, and took a long sip of whiskey. Somehow, her lipstick was still perfect, her freckles still covered with foundation.

"If I ever get as fat as Kristen or as ugly as Corvis," she said, stretching out in Susan's back seat, "just shoot me and dump my body in the South River."

"Only if you promise to do the same for me," I said, reaching for the flask.

I never had to buy my own alcohol.

"Mean," said Susan, and that word hung in the air.

Through the rearview mirror, I watched Heather's bright-red lips curl into an approving smile.

―――――――

About fifteen of us stood at the top of Fourth Cliff, watching the brackish black water thirty-eight feet below.

The water would be freezing, we knew.

I thought of the dead uncle again, and pictured him standing on top of the ocean. *You can be magnificent like me,* he said.

I eyed Brad, who I knew must be terrified. I suspected not only that his thoughts were like elevator music, but also that he might write poetry in secret.

Brad and I shared the quality of no one being allowed to call dibs on us. Or everyone being allowed. That's why Susan couldn't fault me when he asked me to homecoming, even though she wanted to go with him.

Some kids laughed nervously, but I could tell they thought I'd chicken out.

Brad walked up behind me. Even though his tux was wrinkled, he still looked put-together.

"You're not actually doing this, are you?" he asked.

I took off my heels.

"We all are," said Heather. She looked at Brad when she spoke, but she was really talking to me. Since first grade, Heather and I were always daring each other, even when we weren't sure what the dare even was.

Susan grabbed my wrist, holding me back.

You could be magnificent like me.

Everyone watched. I couldn't disappoint them.

When I saw Susan look back at Brad, I knew she wanted to be holding his hand instead of mine. She wanted to stay on the cliff with him, instead of hurling herself off it with me.

"Jump!" Scottie shouted.

I held Susan's hand, and Heather touched my waist with her manicured fingers before taking my free hand in hers.

"You're a genius," she whispered directly into my ear just before we pulled Susan over the edge with us. Susan screamed like a creepy clown was murdering her one limb at a time.

It felt like the air was gone.

I lost my stomach right away, and then again about halfway down.

The water hurt when my bare feet hit, and the cold sucked the breath out of me.

We all surfaced. We did not die.

Susan looked at me with intense anger, but then I wrapped my arms around her, holding her close, and whispered, "We did it" into her cheek.

Heather glanced at the two of us and frowned slightly, then ducked underwater again. When she resurfaced, her dress was floating downriver. She turned to face our classmates, braless, and everyone cheered—Scottie loudest, probably because he was the one who got to touch Heather's boobs. They weren't exactly together, but they definitely had a lot of sex. Both Heather and Susan slept with boys in our grade all the time—Heather was even the one Brad lost his virginity to—and it was hard to keep pretending I didn't feel left out.

"Don't be mad," I whispered to Susan. I wrapped my arm around her back, hoping it felt strong.

Moving toward the shore, holding each other, it felt like my dress weighed eight hundred pounds. I could barely make out the faces of my classmates standing above us, but I heard their soft overlapping voices, full of a kind of subdued cheerfulness, and they began to sound not like people but like the audience of a play. We were onstage, which made Susan's anger dissipate.

The dead uncle was right. I felt different. I felt like I'd gotten away with something, like I'd cheated death.

I hoped that on Monday, Corvis McClellan would notice.

Susan lived in a two-hundred-year-old colonial on Juniper Hill Road, white with black shutters. It was so old that it faced away from the street, reminding us that the street used to go a different way when there were horses and buggies. The staircase had ropes instead of railings, which you held on to when you walked up the steps, and I liked to imagine that the ropes were so old that seamen's wives held them hundreds of years ago when they went to sit in the widow's watch and wait for their husbands to return from sea. I also liked to imagine that those seamen's wives were ghosts now, pacing in circles above our heads, judging our hairstyles and our sex lives.

The Blackfords had a beautiful yard, which was Mrs. Blackford's pride and joy. There were tulips in little clusters, and old wooden lobster traps scattered like chess pieces, with flowers sprouting inside them.

We stepped on the tulips on our way into the house, laughing in our soaking-wet dresses. Heather had gone home with Scottie, and since Brad didn't jump, it was easy to keep up the momentum with Susan, and now it was just the two of us.

Once we got to Susan's bedroom, I felt the rush of the jump leaking out of me. I opened the top drawer of Susan's bureau, searching for pajamas. She kept all kinds of things in there, including notes I'd passed her in American History, origami fortune-tellers Heather had made—each fortune focused on either sex or alcohol—and balled-up silk hair ribbons that she'd worn in ballet recitals. Next to the stack of nightgowns was a small collection of items Brad had touched—a pencil he'd given Susan in middle school, a shoelace from his lacrosse cleats, a tube of ChapStick that Susan had loaned him once. *It touched his lips,* I remembered her saying. I grabbed a nightgown from the top of the stack and pushed the drawer closed.

I changed quickly in the corner and sat down on her bed.

I wondered where Corvis was. Having sex with Kristen in the dunes? Cuddling with Kristen while they watched a silent French film?

Kristen was fat, but she had attitude. Her earrings were safety pins. She was obsessed with whatever political issue was cool that week in the band-and-art-kid crowd. Sometimes it was feminism, sometimes the environment. I'd overheard Kristen in the hallway, saying she was going to join the Earth Liberation Front, but she'd quickly abandoned that in favor of gay rights when her friends changed passions.

They hated us. We hated them. It worked out pretty well.

Sliding out of her wet dress, Susan watched herself in the mirror on the back of the door.

She stood in the perfect first position, a habit from ballet.

She was a good ballerina, with extremely high arches and hyperextended legs. Once, she played Clara in the Boston Ballet production of *The Nutcracker*. She mostly just flitted around the stage in a nightgown that made her look like an exquisite, helpless ghost.

I'd taken ballet as a child, too, but after a while, Sandra could no longer afford the lessons like Susan's parents could, which was a good thing, honestly, because I was thrust into all of the main roles even though I sucked. As we grew, though, Susan's body betrayed her—her chest and hips meant that she could never join a company.

Susan pinched her stomach and sighed, turned, and pinched the other side, measuring the skin between her fingers.

She groaned. "My body has no *drama*."

"What do you mean?" I asked, looking from her head to her feet, which were bruised and scabbed from both toe shoes and heels.

"I don't know," she said, turning and examining herself from the other side again, then looking sharply at my reflection. "Your body is like a secret or something. A secret that Brad wants to find out."

I pulled my knees to my chest, covering myself.

I thought of the night in Brad's Datsun. Then I thought of the herpes.

Susan switched to the fifth position and looked at my reflection in her mirror again. It didn't matter that I wasn't Brad's official girlfriend, because everyone already acted like I was, and eventually I would have to be. He'd asked me to be his homecoming date by leaving flower petals around my locker, which the whole school saw.

"I don't think Brad has any secrets," I said.

"That's why he wants yours," Susan said. "Why didn't you leave with him?"

She peeled off her wet strapless bra, revealing full breasts, and turned to me.

"I'm not ready yet," I said. This was usually my excuse for dodging Brad. I was a virgin. I held on to it because I was afraid, but also because virginity was a powerful thing. It was a way to avoid Brad, to be closer to Susan—a get-out-of-jail-free card—but it was also something you only get one of, and therefore it was valuable.

"It doesn't hurt as much as people say," Susan said. She held it over me sometimes that she'd slept with boys.

"There are different kinds of hurting," I said.

Susan stood in front of her dollhouse, picking up the tiny porcelain father and examining him between her fingers. This wasn't just any dollhouse—it had working crystal chandeliers, parquet floors, and a phonograph that played scratchy-sounding old-timey music. Her grandfather had built it for her mother, who gave it to Susan for her tenth birthday.

"You might as well get it over with, and Brad would be nice," Susan said wistfully, placing the father doll in the upstairs bedroom of the dollhouse. I waited for her to continue, but instead she said, "I'm so tired."

She walked over to her bed, which had little carved pineapples on each corner of the frame, and Laura Ashley sheets that I was sweating on, and lay down next to me. She wore only a clean, dry pair of white cotton underpants. Her damp arm touched mine. She leaned into me, and we were quiet for a while. My foot twitched embarrassingly.

Looking down over her shoulder, I saw a mark from where her

father had hit her with his belt. It stretched across the middle of her back, a smear of fading pink. I imagined that my fingertips were magical, that they could wipe it away like a paper towel in a Mr. Clean commercial. I wanted to touch it, to place my feelings on top of it, but we had a silent agreement that I would ignore marks like these, so I didn't say anything.

Susan was basically sleeping, but she said, "What is it like, being you?"

"It sucks," I said. I moved my arm so that it touched more of hers, but not too much. I was wearing an entire nightgown.

This was the kind of question she only asked me if she'd been drinking. The question could have stemmed from my crown, which she had propped on her naked stomach, or it could have been about Brad. I saw her watching us dance together before I puked in the secret bathroom, and then again when he approached me at Fourth Cliff.

I wondered how Susan managed to get the crown back from whoever rescued it before we jumped. It was pretty busted-up.

She rolled over to face me, fitting her head between my collarbone and my neck. I stiffened.

"Are you okay?" she asked.

Everyone was always asking me that, except for Sandra. I knew they either wanted me to just say yes, to pretend I was always fine — or maybe they wanted to feel powerful by helping me.

Susan's parents hated each other, but she had two of them. I only had one. Sandra was never home, and other than Stephanie Tanner, my goldfish, she was all I had.

"I'm fine," I said. Susan's boob was touching me now, with only the thin cotton of my nightgown between us.

"Am *I* okay?" Susan asked.

"Yes," I whispered.

"I'm cold," Susan said, wrapping an arm around me.

It was an invitation to touch her. I pulled the blanket up around us, and my whole body tingled. This was a feeling that I both loved and hated.

Susan was the kind of girl who clung to other girls' arms in the cold, who borrowed people's coats and burrowed her nose into the neckline, who looked at me with this irresistible helplessness and said, "Keep me warm?"

The weight of her head on my chest made me feel strong, protective, like I mattered, and the smell of her—of baby powder, clean laundry, salt like the ocean—was intoxicating.

Keep me warm?

Hold my hand?

Is it going to be okay?

Yes, I always answered. *Yes, yes, yes.*

Even though I knew I couldn't answer that question, even though I didn't know if any of us would be okay, or even if we were right now.

Yes.

When I said it to Susan, it felt true. It felt like I knew the answers.

What I loved most about her was that in those moments, when I said yes, she believed me.

"I guess maybe I'm not fine," I said after a while, trying it out. "I can't really tell."

But Susan was already snoring into my collarbone, and I didn't want to move. I wanted to keep her there forever. It made me sad that she would eventually roll over or wake up.

"I don't know what to do," I whispered to someone. Maybe to my father.

While other people prayed, I wrote letters to him, though it had been a while since I'd written one. Because he was missing, he held all the possibility of the tooth fairy, of Daniel Boone, of Paul Bunyan, of God.

I was pretty sure my father was Johnny Moon, the movie star who once spent a summer in Hopuonk, filming a movie right around the time I would have been conceived. He was famous for being beautiful—not for choosing good movies—though lately he'd been trying to take on more serious roles. I looked like him, especially in the nose. Other people thought this, too, though they rarely discussed it with me.

Of course he went to The Mooring while he was here, and every man who went to The Mooring fell in love with Sandra. Loving Sandra was just a liability of being around her.

The Full House

When I got home late the next morning, I saw that Brad had let himself into my house. He sat at the kitchen table reading the newspaper. He looked up when the broken screen door slammed against the frame.

"Hey," he said, and held up the front page of the *Hopuonk Mariner*, which showed a photo of Principal Deftose crowning me while I wore the same dress I still had on, but back when it was clean.

Taylor Garland, Hopuonk's sweetheart, the caption said.

"What are you doing here?" I asked.

It infuriated me that Brad felt comfortable enough to just walk into my house. It also infuriated me that he looked well rested, like he'd showered and brushed his teeth.

"I came to check on you," said Brad. "You and Susan disappeared after you jumped last night, and I wanted to make sure you didn't break your ankles."

"I'm fine, Brad," I said, grabbing the newspaper from him and smacking it facedown on the kitchen table. "How long have you been here?"

"You left without saying goodbye," he said. "Where did you go?"

I glared at him, at his shiny chestnut-brown hair and matching eyes, at his single dimple. His smell of Old Spice and safety made me feel like I was in a scene from a 1950s sitcom.

In contrast to him, I smelled like cheap hair spray and salt water, and the inside of my mouth tasted like a mouse had crawled inside it and died. Still, I knew I wouldn't shower for a long time, because I didn't want to wash off the remnants of Susan's baby powder–ocean scent.

"Susan's," I said.

"You were my date," he said, looking at his legs and sliding his hands up and down his thighs. "You could have at least let me drive you home."

I let his comment hang in the air and looked away, watching dust motes swirl around in the dirty-yellow light of my kitchen. It was freezing, because my house wasn't a real house. What I mean is, it wasn't winterized. It was a beach house, meant for vacation.

I shivered.

"Susan was too drunk to drive home," I said—not exactly a lie, but she'd driven anyway. I shrugged, still not looking at him. Out the window, the birds sounded like people pretending to be birds.

"Whatever," he said.

"Did you expect me to just leave Susan at Fourth Cliff?"

"No," he said. "I don't know. Why didn't you let Jake drive her home? He was her date."

"He was even drunker," I said.

"Fine," he said. "I'm sorry."

He poured me a cup of coffee in a chipped mug that had a picture of dinosaurs smoking on it. Under the dinosaurs were the words *The Real Reason Dinosaurs Are Extinct*. Sandra smoked, so the mug was a mystery.

"Just because you were my date doesn't mean I owe you anything," I said. "I told you I'm not ready."

That usually shut him up, because he was a good person. He didn't want to push me.

"I'm sorry," he said again.

I sat at the kitchen table and let the dress bunch into an itchy ball of damp tulle around my legs. *Full House* was on the small television we kept on the counter. Joey did something with Mr. Woodchuck, which activated the laugh track. I thought I recognized some of the laughs from yesterday.

"I'm going to move to LA and be a professional laugher," I said, taking a sip of coffee.

"Is that a thing?" he asked.

I turned to the television, dismissing him. There was something comforting about *Full House*. When I was little, I imagined D.J. touching my hair while I fell asleep on her bed. Now, Stephanie was my favorite, because she was the underdog, and D.J. was too boy crazy in her teenage years.

"The Tanners are lucky that they live in California," I said, not necessarily to Brad. Their house was just like all the others on the street—unlike mine, which was smaller than everyone else's. Behind the city, they had mountains to look at.

I imagined myself in California with Johnny Moon, where no one knew me, and wondered what it would be like to start over.

"The Tanners aren't real," Brad said. He still had this hangdog look on his face, like a bald eagle who'd been caught eating roadkill.

"Are *you* real?" I asked him. There had to be something he was hiding. He couldn't possibly be this even-tempered and satisfied all the time.

He looked confused, like he was attempting to solve a complicated mathematical equation.

"What do you hate?" I asked him.

"*Hate?* I don't know. Biology?"

I wasn't satisfied.

"*Who* do you hate?" I asked.

He shrugged.

"No one," he said. "O. J. Simpson, I guess."

I sighed.

On the kitchen counter, there was a packet from Massachusetts College of Pharmacy and Health Sciences, where I was supposed to apply for a seventeen-month program in dental hygiene. Sandra thought it was a great idea, and so did Mr. Doyle, the guidance counselor at my high school.

I hated going to the dentist, and I couldn't imagine going to one every day for work. It smelled like rubber gloves, artificial mint, and fear.

Sandra had made it clear that I needed to move out after graduating. I was starting to get nervous, because, first of all, I wasn't completely sure that I *would* graduate. My grades were shit. In eighth grade, they separated the smart kids from the regular kids, and out of our group, only Corvis was put in the accelerated classes.

"Is your favorite food oatmeal?" I asked Brad. "Or, like, pot roast?"

I was really cold now. Choosing to put the dress back on had been a mistake, but I didn't know what else to do with it.

"Are you okay?" he asked. He looked like he wanted to carry me somewhere.

"I just want to go back to bed," I said.

I would lie in my bed and close my eyes, imagining that Susan was there with me.

Brad stood to leave, shrugging on his Carhartt jacket. With his hand on the doorknob, he said, "Taylor, you would make an excellent professional laugher."

And then he left, closing the door gently behind him. Brad always did things gently.

I looked back at the television. Whenever one of Johnny Moon's movies came on, I would ask Sandra if she'd met him when he filmed the movie in Hopuonk, and every once in a while, she told me the story of how he'd come into The Mooring. When I asked if they had had a big romantic affair, she did not deny it.

Other kids' fathers left them, but mine didn't even know about me. That glimmer of hope—that he might want to know, that he might let me go live with him in California—that was all I had if I didn't want to be a dental hygienist.

I went upstairs and stood in the doorway of Sandra's room, which smelled like dust, drugstore perfume, and superiority. She faced the wall, her red hair spilling across the faded pillowcase, and a man lay in bed beside her. I couldn't see his face, but his legs were tangled in hers, and he was balding a little.

"I got queen," I said.

Sandra was also the Hopuonk homecoming queen, but in 1978.

She didn't say anything, but I could feel her listening.

Outside, Brad's Datsun crunched over the gravel as he pulled away.

I walked into the bathroom to do my morning ritual. I'd read about it in one of Sandra's issues of *Cosmo*.

Use yourself as perfume, it said in slinking pink cursive. *It drives them wild!*

Watching my reflection, I slid a finger inside myself. I moved it in slow circles, removed it, then dotted my temples with it.

My hair and eyes were just brown, and I tried to figure out what other people thought was so special about me. I remembered something Heather said to me once in the bathroom at school, while she applied frosty lipstick to my lips, and I pictured her voice in the pink cursive from the magazine.

"Your features are impossibly perfect. Everyone wants you, Taylor. Be careful."

The Spiderweb

The next day at work, I spent most of my time grinding coffee beans. Since I was fourteen, I'd been a coffee girl at Emmylou's. Heather worked there too. I was the only employee without blond hair.

Heather arranged a bunch of Saran Wrapped cinnamon buns and neatened the scratch ticket rolls. The top button of her uniform shirt was undone, showing her cleavage.

Emmylou's doubled as a convenience store, with shelves full of instant noodles, one-dose packs of Advil and Pepto-Bismol, and penny candy. We also sold single rolls of toilet paper, expired gum, and last week's issues of the *Hopuonk Mariner* and the *Boston Sunday Globe*. On every copy of the *Mariner* we had in stock, I was featured on the cover.

Brad and Scottie were there, drinking their second cups of coffee, basically harassing us. Brad drank black coffee, but Scottie ordered Twix-flavored, just so he could comment on how disgusting it was. We specialized in coffee that was dessert.

Scottie leaned over the counter, pouting at Heather. He reeked of alcohol. He wasn't even hungover yet—he was still drunk from the night before.

"Come on," he said to her. "Don't be gay. Just let me touch your boobs. Just for one second."

Heather put the Saran Wrap down, crossing her arms over her chest. Since they weren't officially together, Scottie felt like he constantly had to chase her, which she liked.

"Get away from me, fuckass," she said, but she was smiling.

"Three seconds." Scottie pushed because of Heather's smile. "What size are they?" he asked.

Heather answered, "D," and seemed both like she was used to being asked this question and like she didn't necessarily mind answering it.

There was an understanding that only hot girls worked at Emmylou's, and also that they would give free coffee to their friends. The coffee girls were between the ages of fifteen and twenty (I was hired young), but the girls on the older end usually only worked a few shifts, because they were enrolled in beauty school. We appealed mostly to the other high school kids in our social group, middle school girls who wanted to be like us, and dads. The dads were gross.

Half of the fluorescent overhead lighting was broken, giving the whole place a dismal feel. The floor had black-and-white checkered tiles, and everything else—including the walls and ceiling—was hot pink. Our uniform—black booty shorts and pink aprons—went with the walls.

Just then, Corvis walked in with Kristen. My eyes widened

when I saw them—like I said, Emmylou's was understood to be a popular-kid sanctuary. Besides that, Corvis thought the uniforms were sexist. I'd overheard her saying it once.

Scottie noticed them next. He elbowed Brad, cupped his hands over his mouth, and shouted, "Get out, *lesbos!*"

"Come on, man," said Brad. "Shut up."

Corvis looked Scottie straight in the eye and clasped Kristen's hand.

"We just want a cup of coffee," she said.

"Go to Dunkin' Donuts, dyke," Scottie said. He was laughing maniacally, unsteady on his feet.

"Dude," said Brad, elbowing Scottie. "Shut *up.*"

I thought of the note Corvis passed me in seventh grade, and I thought of how she helped me in the bathroom at homecoming, and I wanted to tell Scottie to shut up too.

But I didn't.

Corvis shot me a disapproving look, like she felt sorry for me.

"Come on," she said to Kristen. "Fuck them. Let's go."

"Wait!" I called after Corvis. I didn't mean to say it out loud.

She spun around and looked at me impatiently.

"*What,* Taylor?" she demanded.

There was so much I wanted to say. I didn't want to go with them, but I also did. I was about to ask Corvis to take me with her, but then I felt Heather's eyes on me, and Scottie's, and my heart started pounding.

"Nothing," I said. "Never mind."

I watched their backs as they left, and an elevator in my stomach dropped and kept going, all the way to hell.

"You're an asshole," Brad said to Scottie, who wasn't listening.

Scottie went back to pestering Heather.

Brad shook his head. If I just went ahead and became his girlfriend already, I thought, at least I'd know I was with someone nice, someone way nicer than me.

I pictured our life together, if we had one. Maybe I could get him to switch from Cheerios to Froot Loops. Maybe I could get him to grow his hair out and chop mine off with the edge of his weed whacker. Maybe I could be a landscaper, too, but the kind who shaped bushes into lions and mermaids, and I would own one giant powerful tiller, and one pair of delicate clippers for tails and noses. Maybe Susan could live with us, and we could share her.

"Brad," I said, leaning over the counter. I gestured for him to come close.

Brad leaned in.

"You can be my boyfriend," I whispered into his ear.

————

Later on, just before we closed and the place was dead, Heather finished counting out the cash register and turned to me.

"Wanna go smoke a square?"

"Sure."

We grabbed our peacoats and went out back by the dumpster and sat on the concrete steps. Heather handed me a Salem and lit one for herself. She was going to be a cosmetologist, and she already looked like one. Her makeup was flawless—somehow, her lipstick never rubbed off, and her black eyeliner complemented her eyes, which were bright blue flecked with green.

The next day was payday. I used my checks for gas and things, but the rest went into this empty Russell Stover box, bills laid flat, smelling like chocolate. There was already almost five grand in there—I was saving it in case I needed getaway money. If I stayed, I could spend it on landscaping tools, and on Susan.

Heather spent her checks on makeup and leather boots. She only took the job to solidify her hot-girl status. She didn't need the money. She lived in Arrowhead, where the houses were expensive—way more expensive than the old houses—and you got to choose what went inside them before they were built for you. You could add dishwashers, home theater rooms, in-ground swimming pools, saunas. Heather had a pool *and* a sauna.

We used to play in the woods they chopped down to build the Arrowhead development, and the families who moved into the cheap mansions started to seem garish, like they had no respect for what had once been standing where they stood now, microwaving their vegetables and filling their giant bathtubs.

Heather didn't miss the woods. She preferred her pool and sauna.

"Brad's officially my boyfriend," I said, trying to sound hopeful.

She looked at her feet and sighed, wiping her pumps with the sleeve of her peacoat even though they weren't dirty.

"You really shouldn't be fucking with Brad," she said. "Susan is in love with him, and you aren't."

"What if I am?" I tried to pull down my top to cover more of my stomach, but that only made it show more of my boobs. I crossed my arms over my chest. Those uniforms were the worst.

Heather rolled her eyes. "Whatever."

"He made me a mixtape," I said, hoping I sounded convincing.

I knew that it took a lot of work to make a mixtape, because I made them for Susan all the time. If you owned the CDs, it was a little easier, but there were still songs you had to catch while they were playing on the radio. Rushing to hit the RECORD button almost always meant that the beginning of the song was cut off, and the end was interrupted by the radio voice.

Heather raised her eyebrows at me, taking a drag of her cigarette.

"It doesn't have much variety, though," I said. If you asked me, Brad's mixtape had *way* too much Third Eye Blind on it.

Heather sighed.

"You're making a mistake," she said, "but I guess it'll be fun to watch it go up in flames."

"Just try and tell me you love Scottie," I said.

"That's exactly it," said Heather, nudging my leg with hers. I

32

jumped a little. Her skin was so smooth. "I never said I did. That doesn't matter."

"What do you mean?" I asked. "How can you have sex with him constantly if you don't love him even a little? Or is he just really good in bed?"

I didn't mean to sound judgmental. I was actually curious. I wondered if she had any advice that I could use for Brad. Maybe I didn't need to love him.

"I've never even had an orgasm," she said. "At least, I don't think I have."

"Um, you'd know if you did," I said. "Trust me."

Even though I hadn't had sex, I knew how to give myself an orgasm, so I knew what it felt like. *Cosmo* wasn't completely useless.

"Sometimes it feels good," she said, frowning. "I mean, sometimes there's this kind of, like, building feeling? But it's more for them than it is for me. They just don't know it."

She looked ashamed after she admitted this, and she quickly rearranged her face.

"You'll see what I mean when you do it," she said in a superior voice. She loved reminding me that I was a virgin.

I didn't want to see what she meant. It sounded awful.

I flicked my cigarette into a spiderweb by accident, and then the spider appeared and started picking out each fleck of ash, one at a time, and flinging them away. I felt guilty for ruining its house.

"Look at this spider," I said.

Heather looked.

"Gross," she said.

"It's not gross. It's kind of beautiful."

Heather checked her watch, then looked over at the empty parking lot. There was a boom of faraway thunder but no rain. She lit another cigarette.

"I haven't gone home in three days," she said.

I thought of Heather's dad, who worked at the Gillette office in Boston, and her mom, who made cookies in the afternoon for her three daughters, who were on perennial diets.

"They come look for you?" I asked.

"Nah," said Heather. "They don't care where I am."

"Is that why you're such a bitch?" I asked.

Heather smiled.

"Maybe," she said.

I looked again at the spider, which was never going to be able to get rid of all the ashes. There were too many.

"I made a mess," I said, still looking at the spider.

Heather stood to leave, brushing ashes off her lap.

"Don't worry," she said coolly. "Somebody will clean it up."

The Mall

On Monday morning, I passed Corvis in the hall. We made eye contact, and I looked for something in her face that told me she'd heard about my jump off Fourth Cliff. She carried a large binder and a French textbook. I carried a tiny purse that held a pack of cigarettes and a stick of gum. I smiled at her involuntarily, but she didn't smile back.

I ducked into the secret bathroom and realized, with shame, that I was waiting for Corvis to join me. I wanted to ask her if scissoring was really a thing, and what it was like to have sex with a girl—but I knew that was out of the question.

I didn't know what was wrong with me. What did I want from her? I looked down at the toilet, where a skid mark clung to the bowl beneath the water.

I shuddered, and reminded myself who I was.

I found Susan in study hall and convinced her to skip the rest of the day to go to the Hanover Mall with me to look for Halloween costumes for Heather's party the following week. I hated the mall, but Susan loved it.

We stopped in Abercrombie for something I could wear on my first real date with Brad, even though a week had already passed and I still couldn't bring myself to make a solid plan with him. He called twice, and I hadn't called back. I picked up the phone a couple of times, but my hands started shaking and I placed it back on the receiver.

I watched Susan as she pulled sweaters and button-downs from racks, examined them, and put them back, unsatisfied.

Then I found the perfect skirt—corduroy with plaid lining. I pulled it off the rack and held it up.

"Isn't this sad?" I said. *Sad* meant "cute." Like, so cute it kind of makes you sad. For example, when you see a baby duck and you feel like you're either going to squeeze it to death or cry, so you have to walk away. We'd started saying it, and it spread.

"Oh . . ." Susan said.

"What?"

"I wanted to get that skirt," she said.

It didn't seem like her style. She was more miniskirt than corduroy. This was what always happened—Susan wanted what I had.

"You did?"

"Yeah, I saw it last week with my mom. I was saving for it." Sometimes she added detail to make her lies seem more convincing.

Susan was two sizes bigger than me. She was taller, and I was skinnier. It didn't seem fair that I was skinnier, because I didn't go to the gym like Susan did, or spend hours a day doing ballet, or eat nothing but carrot and celery sticks on Tuesdays and Thursdays. I could tell Susan didn't think it was fair either.

I really wanted the skirt. I barely ever saw clothing I wanted, but I knew Susan would look cute in it. This was also what usually happened—I gave things to her.

I guess I felt guilty—that I wanted her, that Brad wanted me—and also, I wanted her to have things, especially something as small as a skirt.

"Here," I said, holding the skirt out. Without even realizing it, I'd skipped a step. I had picked out her size instead of mine in the first place.

"Come inside," Susan said, calling me into the dressing room with her, but we were sober and I wanted to see her in her underwear too badly.

"I'll wait here," I said.

The preppy guy working there was arranging belts and kept looking over at me.

"Hey," he finally said, jutting out his chin. He looked exactly like one of the models on the posters hanging all over the walls.

"Hi." I looked away.

"You like parties?" he asked.

Do you like socks? I felt like asking him. Parties and socks were both inescapable parts of life—liking them or not liking them didn't matter.

"No," I said. "I hate them."

He held his hands up.

"Jesus," he said. I could feel him staring at my ass. Then he went back to arranging belts.

I saw a slice of Susan's body through the slit in the curtain—her bent kneecap, her hip sliding into the corduroy.

Susan opened the curtain. Standing there in the perfect skirt, she was everything I wanted.

She eyed the belt guy.

"He's cute," she said, "but not as cute as Brad."

"I guess."

"Well?" she asked, spinning around in the skirt.

I stood back, pretended to think. It was tricky business, keeping my secret. You could touch only when it was appropriate—sleeping next to Susan in bed after parties, when we were both drunk, when she said she was cold, or when she cried. Other times, I had to practice a lot of self-restraint.

"You look sad," I said.

We wandered around the mall for a while, Susan's Abercrombie bag whacking her shin as we walked. For the first time, the mall looked trashy to me. The lighting was hospital-bright, and the floor was made of dull-orange fake bricks. Many of the stores were empty, their entryways covered by chrome grates. The food court was sparse, and the few restaurants had neon hamburgers or ice cream cones in front of them, and they were called things like Hamburger World. Abercrombie was one of the only stores left where we actually shopped.

On our way to the pop-up Halloween store, we passed Hot Topic, and I saw Corvis and Kristen inside. Bass-heavy, screaming music blared from the store, which looked out of place next to Yankee Candle. Kristen sorted through a table of black fishnet tights, then she picked up a pair of Doc Martens combat boots and slid her finger along the sole.

"Wait," I said, touching Susan's forearm. "Can we stop in Hot Topic?"

Susan looked at me like I suggested we make out with a dead fish.

"*Why?*"

"Halloween costumes," I said.

"I promise we won't find anything there," she said. "Plus, they might murder us for even walking through the door."

She waved a hand at our pastel-colored sweaters and tight jeans, our frosted lipstick, our straightened hair—none of it belonged in Hot Topic.

"We might," I said, pulling her inside. With her arm in mine, I hid behind a tall rack of faux-leather jackets and watched Corvis and Kristen.

"What are we looking at?" Susan said, fidgeting.

"Shh." The horrible music beat in my chest.

Corvis, who didn't see us, ran her fingertips along Kristen's thick waist. I couldn't stop looking. It was almost like watching a fire burn—dangerous and mesmerizing.

"You should get them," said Corvis. She looked kind of out of place too. Clearly, they were shopping for Kristen, who wore necklaces that looked like pit-bull collars.

"I don't know," said Kristen. "They're expensive."

Kristen turned and eyed the kid behind the register, who was in our grade but whose name I'd probably decided not to remember on purpose. His head was shaved, except for a Manic Panic bright-green Mohawk, and he had half-inch plugs in his ears. He was short and too thin, but his demeanor—confident and slightly annoyed, not unlike Heather—insisted on attractiveness despite these physical shortcomings.

"I really think they're going to murder us," Susan whispered. "Can we get out of here?"

"Just wait," I whispered back, elbowing her.

Corvis turned and eyed the register kid, too, then slid her arm all the way around Kristen's waist and kissed her on the side of the neck. I could not *believe* she did that in public.

"I'll get them for you," she said, picking up the boots.

As I watched the three of them while Corvis paid, I saw the slightest exchange between Kristen and the register kid. It was almost undetectable, her high-pitched giggle, the way she let her hand linger for a millisecond longer than necessary when he handed her the bag, but I saw it. Corvis must have too.

"Come on," said Corvis. "I'll get you some cheese fries."

The more I watched, the more I saw that we were both fighting some kind of losing battle. "Never mind," I whispered to Susan. "Let's go."

When we got far enough away from Hot Topic, Susan asked, "Why were we watching Corvis McClellan and Kristen Duffy? Why do you care about them?"

"I don't," I said.

She narrowed her eyes.

"I'm just trying to find a costume for Heather's party," I insisted. I recognized the defensiveness in my voice. "I don't give a fuck about them."

I only really gave like seven fucks, but they were all very obsessive.

As we walked into the pop-up Halloween store, full of cheap, slutty costumes, I decided I would buy one that covered my boobs. I went silent, wondering what the hell I would say to Brad at the party, and if he would corner me into planning a date.

"Are you okay?" Susan asked.

The Real Slim Shady

I tried to convince Susan to go to Salem with me for Halloween, because the witch museum was supposed to be decorated with skulls and fake spiderwebs. Plus, I heard they had actual witches there who could cast spells that worked; maybe they knew one that could make me straight. But Susan wouldn't go, because of Heather's party. I considered ditching the party—maybe trying to convince everyone to break into the abandoned tuberculosis hospital in the woods—but then Susan called three times to ask where I was, so I gave in.

I was pissed-off, so I tossed the costume I'd bought with Susan at the mall and dressed as a s'more. It was easy—Sandra had most of the supplies already. My hair was teased and spray-painted red and orange, with about a gallon of gold glitter in it, so it looked like fire.

"You've got a *pillow* around your waist," Susan said when I got there. She was wearing a sexy Little Bo-Peep outfit, and her entire torso was exposed, even though it was only forty-five degrees.

"So?"

"A pillow," she said again, shaking her head.

Standing on Heather's porch, I heard a loud screech coming

from somewhere else in Arrowhead, near the woods. Susan heard it too. I followed the sound with my eyes. By the edge of the clearing, close to the one house with a gigantic three-car garage, where a trash can had been overturned in the driveway. I saw a raccoon trying to carry an entire package of bologna up a tree. He kept dropping it, but he wouldn't give up.

I felt like that raccoon. Like, I wanted the entire package of bologna *and* I wanted it at the top of the tree.

"Ew!" Susan said, squirming and gripping my arm. "Look at that raccoon!"

The hairs on my arms stood when she touched me, and I wished we could just go home together.

"Raccoons shouldn't be eating bologna," I said absently, watching him try to carry it up the trunk again.

Susan spotted a group of lacrosse players and started tugging me toward them, but I pulled away.

"Where's the keg?" I asked.

Susan pointed toward the back porch.

The living room was full of people, and already a vase had been broken, the jagged pieces of it forgotten on the rug. Through the sliding glass door that led to the manicured yard, I saw kids in slutty costumes crowded around the keg, laughing, holding each other around their waists, slapping each other on the back, stepping in Mrs. Flynn's garden. I went to school with a bunch of kids who got great pleasure out of destroying things.

I headed for the porch.

"Taylor!" someone called. "Come do a shot with us!"

I ignored whoever it was.

It was hard, weaving through a crowd while wearing giant cardboard graham crackers, but at least I wasn't cold. I got a Solo cup and left the porch immediately. All the people made me nervous. When I got back inside, I sat on the couch next to Heather, who was dressed as a sexy French maid.

"A pillow?" Heather said, with a frustrated look on her face. "What exactly are you trying to hide?"

"It's the wrong weather for those costumes," I said. "You think you look sexy, but you just look cold."

Looking around, I saw that every single guy was dressed like Eminem: white guys in white tank tops, white hats, too-baggy jeans.

"God," I said to Heather. "Those costumes."

She smirked. Tonight, her blond hair was curled and her lipstick was blood red. Heather's makeup was perfect. She was especially talented with eyebrows. She crossed one long leg over the other and touched her bottom lip suggestively.

"Who's the real Slim Shady, do you think?" she asked, looking out at the room.

"Where's Brad?" I asked Heather. I tried to seem interested, like I wanted to see him, but really I wondered if I would have to make out with him. The cardboard graham crackers were partially to make that more difficult.

"He has strep throat. Didn't you know?"

"Oh," I said.

Brad and I still hadn't spoken properly since I told him we could be together. So far, we'd smiled at each other in the hallway and that was it. Actually, we were talking less than usual. I knew what was expected of me, and I wasn't sure I could go through with it.

Scottie danced his way over and put one arm around each of us. His eyelids were at half-mast, and he reeked of whiskey.

"Taylor's here," he said. "Now the party can actually get started."

Halloween could have been the best holiday, where you would get to smear fake blood all over yourself and bob for apples, and everything felt a little bit scary, and ghosts were definitely real. Instead, everyone wanted to show off their bodies and play beer pong.

"Yeah, you guys are lame, just sitting around like this," I said, squeezing out from under Scottie's arm.

A terrible song was playing, and everyone sat in clusters. I cupped my hands around my mouth and shouted, "Why aren't any of you assholes dancing?"

Being Taylor Garland meant you always had to be the first to dance.

Even if you didn't feel like dancing.

Even if you just wanted to go home.

I danced as crazy as I could, flapping my arms and shaking my ass, and everyone followed me. I got really into it, and eventually I was so sweaty that I almost forgot about Brad and Susan, and Massachusetts College of Pharmacy and Health Sciences.

I found Susan and pulled her into the middle of the crowd. She held my hands while she danced with me, and I let myself enjoy it. I almost wished I didn't have the pillow around my stomach.

Even though Heather glared at me all night—maybe because she was jealous that I was Brad's girlfriend—I knew she was glad I was there, if only because I got people moving.

I reached out and touched Susan's dark hair, and when I put an arm around her waist, she didn't move away.

———

On the way home, I slowed down in front of Corvis's house and stopped just far away enough so that no one could see me from inside. I turned off my headlights and looked through Corvis's bedroom window on the first floor.

Scream played on her television—it was the very beginning, where Drew Barrymore ran around the house, gripping the telephone. The only light in Corvis's room came from a neon-pink lava lamp. Kristen was there, too, and they were dancing their faces off and eating giant Pixy Stix. There was no beer pong for Corvis and Kristen. They danced like they weren't hiding.

If I stayed home on Halloween with my best friend, the world would stop turning. My phone would ring and ring until I finally showed up, so I wouldn't be able to enjoy any of it. Plus, Susan would never stay home with me in the first place.

Then I heard the cars crunching over gravel. Drunk, stupid voices.

"Hey, it's Taylor's car!" someone shouted. "Guess she thought of it first!"

Scottie's pickup truck pulled in next to my ancient Volvo, screeching to a stop. I saw Heather's face through the glass of the shotgun window, and PJ's face in the back seat. Then another car pulled in, and another.

Like I was saying, parties dissipated quickly when I left, and Brad wasn't there to keep it going for me.

Scottie, red-faced, ran over and pounded on my window. I rolled it down, and a gust of freezing air blew in.

"What are you doing?" I whisper-shouted. I don't know why I was whispering—everyone else was yelling. I glanced at Corvis's window, and this time, she looked back. I'm sure she didn't see my face in the darkness, but she had to see that her street was full of cars and people.

Scottie held up a carton of eggs.

"It's not a good Halloween if you don't egg someone's house," he said. "Come on."

Susan walked behind him, a nervous expression on her face. I got out of the car, and she grabbed my forearm.

"Why did you leave?" she asked me. She was shivering uncontrollably in her tiny costume, her teeth chattering.

We watched as they started throwing eggs at Corvis's car. It was like a nightmare—a bunch of guys in Eminem costumes with cartons and cartons of eggs, laughing like monkeys.

"Happy Halloween, *dyke!*" Scottie shouted.

Heather pulled a package of toilet paper out of Scottie's trunk, and people started throwing that too—all over the house.

"Here, Taylor!" Heather ran up to me and handed me a roll.

I could have stopped them. All I would need to do is call them fuckasses and tell them to go home. They would listen. Their hearts weren't really even in it—they were just drunk and bored. Usually, we did this to Principal Deftose's house. Scottie had probably thought of Corvis because she'd stopped in Emmylou's the other day, or maybe Heather had suggested it. Either way, if I told them to stop, they would.

But I couldn't. What if they suspected I was a homo too?

If Brad were here, he would have stopped it. I knew, in that moment, that he was a better person than I was. I pictured a graph, where a line indicated how good each person was, and my score, just like on the standardized math test, was way below the red line that said you should be at least *here*.

I dropped the roll of toilet paper. Everyone's voices, though they were right beside me, sounded muted, like I was underwater.

I watched Corvis come to the front door and open it. I watched her scream that she would call the cops if we didn't leave, and I watched an egg land on her shoe.

Dyke.

The word bounced around in my head, echoing.

I shrunk back against my car next to Susan, hoping Corvis wouldn't see me. The word *cops* sort of scared everyone, and they started backing off.

"Come on, Susan," I said. "Let's get out of here."

One last look at Corvis showed me that she wasn't crying. She just stood in the doorway, daring them to throw another egg.

The Unicorn

W hen I got home, Sandra sat at the kitchen table, drinking whiskey on ice from a coffee mug. She'd changed from her work clothes into a white terry-cloth bathrobe, but she hadn't taken her makeup off. With her hair down, kinky from the bun she wore at The Mooring, and her lips still stained red, she looked beautiful and mournful. But her nose, a perfect ski-jump, didn't match mine.

"Happy Halloween," I said in a deflated voice. I couldn't get the image of Corvis in her doorway out of my mind.

"What are you supposed to be?" Sandra asked, and the question seemed like a thousand questions wrapped into one.

"A s'more."

Sandra shot me a disapproving look, but she still poured me a cup of coffee to prevent a hangover. I joined her at the table and realized that one of Johnny Moon's movies was playing on the countertop television. I followed her gaze, to a frame of him driving through an unimaginable desert, and I wondered if that landscape could possibly exist.

"How's Brad?" she asked, her eyes never leaving the screen.

"Sick," I said. "Strep."

"Why aren't you taking care of him?" she asked.

"I don't want strep," I said. "Sandra?"

"What?"

"What was it like when you met him?" I asked. "Johnny Moon."

"If you're not careful," said Sandra, "you'll lose him."

I needed to call Brad back. I knew I needed to call him back.

I watched Johnny Moon park the car recklessly and pull a handgun out of his pocket.

In addition to writing letters, I sent Johnny Moon a wallet-sized school photograph every year, but I didn't know if he got any of them, because I just used the fan mail address.

I told him about school being closed for an entire week in fifth grade, when we had that giant blizzard. I told him about how Susan wanted a baby so badly that she walked around her bedroom pretending to breastfeed her stuffed panda bear.

Johnny Moon was kind of like a diary to me, but then one day, I got angry with him for ignoring me, sick of receiving only printed-out photographs with fake signatures on them in return, and I never wrote again. I was not the kind of person who was supposed to act desperate.

"You lose people all the time," I said to Sandra. "You *love* losing people."

"I don't love losing people," she said. "It's just been a while since I've found a man I didn't want to shake off." She pulled the glass ashtray closer and lit a cigarette.

I imagined these men as loose pieces of sand in her shoes, which she shook off before entering the house. But Johnny Moon wasn't sand; he was sea glass.

Still looking at the screen, in kind of a desperate voice, I asked, "Is he my father?"

She looked at me, holding her cigarette to her lips, smoke curling out of her nostrils like a dragon. When she pulled her hand away, the filter was dotted with red lipstick.

"Honey, I've told you—I don't know who your father is."

"But did you know Johnny Moon?" I asked.

"Yes," she said, tossing her hair. "I did."

"What was he like?" I asked, which I knew was a little bit dangerous. This could either work in my favor or cause us to get in a giant fight. When I asked questions about my father, it made Sandra feel bad about herself, and she usually took it out on me. She criticized my hair or makeup, told me I was gaining weight, or just plain ignored me. It didn't help, I'm sure, that I was dressed as a s'more.

"You know," she said. "He was a movie star. He showed up, got everyone excited, then disappeared."

"But what was he *like*?"

"Taylor," she said, "he was like a unicorn."

The Game

Susan and I spent the summer between fifth and sixth grade out in the woods behind my house, pretending to be pirates.

No one else was invited.

We dyed my old bedsheets with coffee and made dirty-looking clothing out of them, braided our hair, and didn't wear shoes.

We built elaborate forts and covered them with moss, pretending they were ship cabins, and wrapped tiny twigs in maple leaves for dinner, with a handful of baneberries on the side. Those were poisonous, so we only pretended to eat them. Sometimes I stole whiskey from Sandra's unlocked liquor cabinet and we each took a sip, calling it liquid courage.

I always chose to be Blackbeard, coloring my chin with Sandra's black eyeliner and bragging about my fourteen wives, of whom I pretended Susan was my favorite. She was Rachel Wall, the only female pirate in New England. In real life, they weren't alive at the same time, but we didn't care.

I remember one night very clearly. It was mid-July, and I didn't want to go inside because Sandra had a man over, a man who I disliked more than the others because he was always slapping my butt or tousling my hair, calling me "my little monkey" and trying to get me to kiss his cheek. Susan sat by the edge of the firepit, tired and swatting at mosquitoes. She wanted to play that we had a baby, and I wasn't interested in that, but I needed to keep her outdoors with me.

I stood, narrowing my eyes, rearranging my face into what I hoped was a brave, serious expression.

"Someone has ravaged our ship," I said, standing at the edge of the forest, wearing one of Sandra's leather boots as a fake leg. I pointed in the direction of my house, accusing Sandra and her boyfriend. "Call for help!" I shouted. "We have to kill them before they make you dance the hempen jig!" One of our favorite facts about Rachel Wall, besides that she was a girl, was that she confessed to practicing piracy just before she was hanged in Boston.

Susan ran into the clearing, screaming at the top of her lungs, then swooning on the ground.

"Help!" she cried before she fell.

I swooped in and killed the invisible enemies with a stick I used as a sword. Susan followed along.

"Die, scallywags!"

We ran around until we were sweating, our cheeks red.

"We must spend the night looking out," I told her when we'd finished killing the enemies. "Let's stay in the crow's nest."

We climbed into the fort and lay down on the blanket stowed inside it, pretending this was the very top of the ship. She laid her head on my stomach, and I put my hand in her hair. We were both breathing heavily, sticky with sweat.

"I will keep watch," I said. I handed her a lime from inside my house, to prevent scurvy. We always carried limes.

Susan took the lime and closed her eyes, and I tangled my fingers in her hair.

"Let's weigh anchor in the morning," I whispered. *Let's get out of here, just you and me.*

"Aye," she answered. "Give me another lime."

Her breathing became deep and steady, and I felt like the leader of the forest. I would stay awake all night, just in case.

———

Now, at yet another one of Scottie's parties, Susan was holding a plastic bottle full of vodka and cranberry juice. We sat on the porch swing, waiting for Brad to arrive. Earlier that day, I answered the phone when he called, panicking slightly at the sound of his voice—the voice of my boyfriend. He asked if I'd be at this party, and I knew it was probably in my head, but his tone made me think it was a dare.

"Remember when we used to play pirates?" I asked Susan.

"What made you think of that?" she asked.

I was always remembering things no one else did and reminding them of these things when they didn't want to be reminded.

"I don't know," I said.

The grass of Scottie's lawn was dim blue in the dark, and the rich, horsey smell of it made me think of playing pirates. It was late fall, though, not summer, and cold. The mosquitoes were long gone, and everything looked smaller than it had that summer when we were eleven.

I took a sip of my beer.

"Sometimes I wish we could still play games," I said. "I just . . . This isn't fun." I was a little drunk.

I saw Brad's Datsun pulling up, him getting out. His lacrosse letterman jacket had a big cartoonish face of a sailor on the sleeve and his last name embroidered on the breast pocket. We were the Hopuonk Beachcombers.

Beachcombers were people who spent their lives roaming the sand, looking for something of value. Often, they'd been banished from pirate ships. Brad's letterman jacket and Heather's cheerleading uniform had the Beachcomber emblem sewed on. Hopuonk's sailor version was actually nothing like what a real beachcomber was—someone who wasn't a sailor at all.

"You're so weird," Susan said, pulling away from me at the sight of Brad.

I had a brief but fierce urge to pull Susan into the bathroom and tell her right then that I was a lesbian, to exonerate myself no matter what the consequences were, but then Brad was in front of me and I could see frustration in his face.

"Hey," I said to him, standing. My head barely reached his shoulder, and he leaned down and kissed my hair.

"You look beautiful," he said, holding me at arm's length, his hands on my shoulders, trying to look cool in front of everyone — in front of Heather. "It's nice to see you."

Even though his words were plain, I felt a little threatened. Because I'd been ignoring him, I'd need to make up for it, and since I wasn't supposed to lose him, I knew that probably meant sex. Sandra said I had to make sure I didn't lose him. I thought about what Heather had said outside Emmylou's — that I wasn't in love with him — and I hated that she was right.

"Let's go upstairs," I said, leaning into him.

As we ascended the stairs, I could feel Susan's eyes on my back.

Heather watched too. I wondered if she was also in love with Brad, if that was why she was so mean.

I was glad that they saw us, but that feeling went away once the door closed. I hated Scottie's bedroom immediately and wondered how Heather spent tons of time here. His bed was dirty and he only had one pillow, but he had three bongs. The cowboy wallpaper on the walls was dingy and covered in posters of barely clothed women, and one with the rules of Beirut that said GET YOUR BALLS WET! across the bottom in neon orange.

"Why have you been ignoring me?" Brad said, now that we were alone. The desperation in his voice made me want to slap him. He was the captain of the lacrosse team. Every girl wanted him. Susan wanted him. He was supposed to be confident, to know where to put his hands.

"I'm not ignoring you," I managed to say.

He was right, though.

"You're supposed to be my girlfriend," he said, as if he were reading my mind.

Starting in middle school, my friends would get upset about boys. They cried in bathrooms at dances, they held hands with boys in the hallway, and they wrote their initials next to the initials of whoever they had a crush on, with little hearts around them.

I'd tried having boyfriends—I even agreed to go out with Scottie in eighth grade, then avoided him until finally dumping him at a school dance. I just couldn't muster up the same emotions as my friends. It was around that time I knew something was wrong with me.

"Aren't you?" said Brad. "Still my girlfriend?"

His voice sounded like a child asking to sleep in his mother's bed after a nightmare.

"Yes," I said, trying to be kind. "I'm still your girlfriend. I'm sorry I didn't call you back. I'm not sure how to do this girlfriend thing."

He took my agreement as permission. He reached for me and kissed me, very gently. Still, his stubble scratched my chin, and it hurt.

Then he stepped out of his pants and put his hands on my thighs. I watched his every move, trying to learn from him, to learn what it was that Susan loved.

I thought of eleven-year-old Susan's sleeping face as he pushed his body against me. That face was so far away.

Before I knew it, he'd tugged his boxers off, and there it was: his penis, which looked like a floppy joystick. He reached for the button on my jeans. I was still fully clothed.

I slid out of my jeans and pulled my sweater over my head, tossing it on the floor. He pressed his body against mine.

Brad was breathing heavily now, and he slid his hand under the elastic band of my underpants. No penetration had occurred when, suddenly, he froze, his face white, and I felt moistness on my thigh.

Oh my God. Gross. Gross!

"Oh . . . okay," I said. I knew that I wasn't supposed to reassure him. It would make both of us feel worse.

I needed a shower. I wanted to take about seventeen showers, and put on the cleanest pajamas in my bureau.

At least this meant I wouldn't have to do it with him.

"I . . . Sorry," he mumbled. And then he was pulling his boxers back on, followed by his pants.

"I'll call you more from now on," I said miserably, but he was already halfway out the door.

I felt a wave of nausea so huge that I leaned back on the bed without even getting dressed. Everything was spinning.

"Susan!" I shouted. I doubted she could hear me over the music downstairs, but I shouted her name again and again, and finally she appeared in the doorway.

Susan came over and sat on the edge of the bed, leaning over me. Her black hair spilled onto my chest. She placed a palm on my forehead, but there was still resentment in her expression.

"Did you guys do it?" she asked.

"I don't feel good," I said.

"What do you need?" she said absently.

My nausea passed. I blinked.

"A lime," I said.

The Note

I left Scottie's party with six rolls of stolen toilet paper in my bag, then drove to Corvis's house.

I saw that only her car was in the driveway—her parents' old Subaru Outback, recognizable because of the bumper stickers Corvis had plastered all over the back. Leaving my bag in the car, gathering the rolls of toilet paper in my arms, I walked to the front door and rang the bell with my elbow.

When Corvis opened the door, she looked surprised to see me, but not that surprised.

"Hi," I said.

She raised an eyebrow. Her jeans were ripped, and she wore a faded T-shirt that said FREE PALESTINE, which made me feel stupid, because I didn't know anything about Palestine or why it wasn't already free.

"What are you doing here?" Tucked under her arm was a book by someone named Virginia Woolf. I liked that name—it sounded like the name of a famous dead female pilot or an incredibly sexy double-jointed circus performer.

"Listen," I said. "I was here the night everyone egged your house.

I mean, I showed up first—I don't even know why—but I was still here when everyone messed up your house, and I didn't stop them, and I'd really like it if you'd get me back."

She shifted her weight from one leg to the other and leaned against the door frame. Her socks had little tacos on them.

Sandra's face popped into my mind—her languid, distant who-cares face. I looked at Corvis desperately. *Punish me*, I thought. Please *punish me*.

"I'm sorry for everything I did in seventh grade," I said, "and everything I didn't do since then. I'm an asshole. Look, I even brought supplies."

I held out a roll of toilet paper, persistent, and she said, "Stop."

"No, I'm serious," I said. "Mummy me."

At middle school dances, I cried in the bathroom sometimes, just like the other girls, but for different reasons.

Once, at the beginning of seventh grade, I was dancing with Mike O'Malley, and his touch made me feel sick, so I ran away, leaving him on the dance floor.

Corvis found me in the bathroom.

"I didn't mean to," I said, crying. "I didn't mean to leave him there."

She pulled some toilet paper from one of the rolls and brushed the tears from my cheeks.

"I know," she said.

She looked at me a little too long. Lately, I'd started to see similarities between Corvis and me. We both loved Drew Barrymore and Madonna just a bit too much. Susan and Heather loved them, too, but then their posters switched to shirtless boys from Abercrombie magazine ads, while Corvis and I both kept Drew Barrymore and Madonna on our bedroom walls.

"I don't want to dance with them either," she admitted.

I stopped crying. The toilet paper she'd given me was moist now and wadded in my fist.

The bathroom was gross. Girls drew their names and hearts all over the mirror with lipstick, and no one washed it off. There were carvings of penises in the metal of the stalls, tampon wrappers on the floor, unidentifiable stains everywhere. In the middle of the room, there was a drain, stopped up by hair.

Why was it that our only place to hide had to be so disgusting?

"What's wrong with me?" I said.

"Nothing's wrong with you," said Corvis, just as Susan and Heather burst in.

"What's *wrong* with you?" Heather demanded, her hands on her hips. She was wearing flared jeans and a tiny shirt. "Why did you leave Mike there like that?"

"He's really embarrassed," said Susan. She wore a baby-doll dress with a white cotton T-shirt underneath, her black hair braided.

Corvis stepped in front of me. "Taylor is really embarrassed too."

"I'm fine," I said. "Mike just smells like cheese puffs."

Corvis shot me a look. Heather and Susan started laughing, and from that point on, Mike O'Malley was known as Cheese Puff Boy.

The following Monday at school was when Corvis passed me the note.

We were sitting in study hall—Corvis had already been put in accelerated, so this was our only period together other than lunch.

Brad was there too. His math book was open on the desk in front of him—a desk too small to hold him already. His legs stretched out in all directions, the laces on his Pumas untied. He looked at the book like it was written in Chinese.

PJ elbowed me—I'd been staring at Brad, wondering what it would be like to have such long legs—and handed me the note.

I unwrapped it—it was folded into an origami fortune-teller, a disguise—and it read, *Do you think about girls the way Susan thinks about Brad?—C*

Underneath, she'd drawn three boxes, for me to check one: *Yes*, *No*, or *Maybe*.

I felt my cheeks burning.

I knew the answer, but I shoved the note into my pocket.

I made eye contact with Corvis for a millisecond, then looked away.

What I did afterward was unforgivable, yet I felt I had no choice. Notes were supposed to be sacred. I was about to break the girl code.

———

"I don't really see the point," Corvis said now, wrapping me in toilet paper. I spun around, to make it easier for her, and lifted my arms so she could reach my armpits.

"The point is that I deserve to be punished," I said.

"Yeah, but you seem to be enjoying this," said Corvis. She stood back, frowning and assessing her work.

We stood on the faded Turkish rug in her bedroom, our feet surrounded by books, pencils, and glassblown pipes filled with charred remnants of weed. The names on the spines of Corvis's books were unrecognizable to me, but enticing: Maya Angelou, Simone de Beauvoir, bell hooks, which wasn't capitalized for some reason. I liked all of their names better than mine.

"Maybe we need to add eggs to this equation," I said.

"What are you trying to do?" she asked. "What do you want?"

I looked at her face, noticed that her skin was blotchy in certain places and pale in others, and had a passing thought that Heather would suggest a toner to clear it up. Corvis's pale, almost nonexistent eyebrows needed plucking. Loose, wild hairs escaped her ponytail.

"I don't know," I said. "That's the problem."

She sighed.

"I'm just really sorry," I said, "and it won't be any good if I don't go out in public like this. Let's go to the grocery store and buy some eggs, and you can crack them over my head."

I moved toward the doorway, but she grabbed my arm and looked at me, hard.

"My car, then?" I asked. "Do you want to throw them at my car instead?"

"Taylor," she said, exasperated. "You're being pathetic."

I sighed.

"I keep meaning to be a different person," I said.

"Come into the kitchen," she said. "I'll make us hot chocolate, but don't tell anyone about this. Kristen would make so much fun of me if she knew we were hanging out."

The Lacrosse Helmet

As soon as I told Sandra that Brad was officially my boyfriend, she took me to get birth control.

The gynecologist was cool enough not to let on that she'd seen me before, and I left with a plastic case full of little circles, one for each day. I would take them every morning at seven o'clock, just before I left for school.

If I was going to have sex with Brad, at least I wouldn't get pregnant.

I still couldn't really understand sex, or how people just *had* it. I mean, obviously I knew what it *was*, because Sandra told me in kindergarten. What I couldn't understand was how people could bring themselves to just be naked in front of another person like that, and then let someone go *inside* them.

The word *had* was weird, even, because it's like people were saying that sex was something you could own, like a lawn mower or a toaster oven.

Anyway, when Brad went down on me in his Datsun—not even bringing the herpes into it, but just the act itself—it made me feel like he was disgusting. He was disgusting for wanting to do that to me, and I was disgusting for letting him. I couldn't even watch—I just moaned after what felt like forever, and he stopped. Then I was supposed to pretend it was the greatest thing in the world. Like, *Oh my God, I'm so grateful.*

Heather had sex all the time—lots of times with people she barely knew. I could tell she usually felt bad afterward, but it also gave her this sort of power that you could see—like she had discovered a lost island.

Heather was the one that Brad lost his virginity to—in the cabin of Scottie's father's sailboat, while it was tied up to the dock at Humming Rock. Susan had sex too. Some of the people they'd had it with overlapped, since Hopuonk was such a small town.

Even Corvis had sex, at her summer camp in Maine. It was all girls, and Corvis had sex with more than two of them. I overheard her talking to Kristen about it once in the locker room. She also had sex with at least one girl at Lilith Fair—that weird feminist music festival—last summer, right after the Indigo Girls played. Unlike Heather, she didn't appear to feel bad about it. She just did it.

I think everyone knew I was a virgin, but they didn't know I had an STD.

The word *herpes* sounds like the thing it is.

On the car ride home from the gynecologist, I could tell Sandra was proud of me. Having sex meant you were normal. "So you and Brad are really together?"

She could come to LA too, I thought. *She could have a diamond-*

encrusted toothbrush, a sports car made of pure gold, a face that was known by people. I could give those things to her, if Johnny Moon wanted me. I could give those things to her, and to Susan, and they would love me. What could I give her here? A red-faced, crying grandchild? A spare room in a Cape house when she grew too old to bartend—a room swirling with dust and sadness? Clean teeth every six months?

"We're really together." Saying it out loud, I felt both regret and relief that I had a cover. I turned the idea over and over in my mind, trying to find a version of my life with Brad that felt okay, but all I came up with was a house with electric heat, and possibly a baby pretty enough for Sandra to love.

Sandra adjusted her sunglasses, checked herself in the rearview mirror. Satisfied with her own face, she glanced at the reflection of mine.

"Sometimes," she said, "I wondered if you were . . . Never mind."

I swallowed. "Wondered if I were what?" We passed the old drive-in hamburger joint where the waitresses used to wear roller skates to deliver food to the cars, before it closed down. We passed the depressed downtown of Hopuonk, mostly boarded-up, and a middle-aged Irish couple walking into the drugstore, their matching bright-red hair blowing in the wind.

"If you were a lesbian," she finally said.

My eyes went wide at the thought that she noticed me enough to catch on.

"Well, Brad's my boyfriend," I said.

I thought of the eggs hitting Corvis's house.

I'd heard lots of lesbians lived in California. The problem was, I didn't have an escape plan. I'd saved all of my money from Emmylou's, but I didn't know what to do with it. I had a car, but I didn't know where to go in it. An anchor was tied to my ankle, and I gripped the box of birth control like a parachute.

If I stayed in my Hopuonk snow globe, maybe it wouldn't be that bad, I thought, trying to convince myself. Sandra would be proud of me, and Brad was a good person. We could swim in the ocean and have salty threesomes with Susan. Who else would she marry? Mostly, Brad would watch. I knew she wanted him and not me, but maybe she would take me along with him. Gradually, he could become like the gardener, or a beloved grandfather clock, a permanent but forgotten fixture in the living room—comforting, useless, and pretty.

"I'm going to be so terrible at being a dental hygienist," I said. "I'm failing algebra. And biology." I wanted Sandra to know that just because I got queen, things weren't solved.

Mr. Sheehan pulled me aside after class the other day, a concerned-teacher expression on his face. He told me I probably needed summer school if I wanted to graduate, and he wouldn't look me in the eye.

"Oh, I failed algebra too," Sandra said.

I wanted her to sound more worried. I wanted her to punish me.

"Honey, I've heard you getting sick in the bathroom," Sandra said, staring at the broken stoplight on Main Street, which stayed red for at least ten minutes at a time.

I was ashamed—it was disgusting, how I got sick all the time.

"You're not already pregnant, are you?" Sandra asked. "Because if you are, we can . . . take care of it."

"No," I said. "I just . . . sometimes when I'm really nervous, it makes me sick."

Sandra's shoulders settled, and she loosened her grip on the steering wheel.

"Don't be embarrassed," she said. "It's okay to do that sometimes. You know, when you've overeaten. Just don't do it *too* much, okay?"

Oh. That's what she thought.

"Okay, Sandra," I said. The magnitude of what she didn't understand was so big that I couldn't say anything else.

———

The thing about it was, Brad wasn't as bad as I thought he would be. Especially if I imagined us both becoming landscapers.

The first time we hung out alone, Brad and I were lying in his bed, and I let him hold my hand. That part, I didn't mind so much. I held his back, the birth control swirling around in my body somewhere, protecting me. He had small, delicate hands, and womanish lips.

Both of us had decided to pretend that what happened in Scottie's bedroom didn't happen, in the interest of protecting our dignity. I could hear Sandra's words — *if you're not careful, you'll lose him* — and I desperately wanted to like him back.

"You can hold my hand in school, too, if you want," I said.

"Okay," he said.

His comforter was Eddie Bauer plaid, his sheets matching. His closet overflowed with lacrosse equipment.

I was wearing the helmet, as both a joke and a barrier.

"I'm failing biology," I said, trying this fact out on him. "I don't get what a spleen even does."

He said, "I know, right?"

"And I don't want to know, like, at all," I said. The helmet muffled my voice.

He squeezed my hand. I didn't hate it.

"I don't think of myself as a person who really even has a spleen. Or a pancreas," he said.

A moment passed, and in that moment, I imagined myself without skin, without a body, as only a spine with wings attached, bleached white, beating above the clouds. If that were true, I would not be Taylor Garland. My name would be made of syllables only the wind could pronounce.

"I don't think I'm going to graduate," I said, "which means I won't get into Massachusetts College of Pharmacy and Health Sciences, which means I'm literally a moron."

"It's okay to be afraid," he said, and I wondered what his biggest fear was. "I have a D in biology."

I adjusted the helmet and sat up, facing him.

"I am a Soviet pilot," I said.

He shoved me.

"I am a deep-sea welder," I said. "My name is Walter Bronstein. I only eat raw eggs."

He pinched my waist, and I shoved him away, laughing.

"I am an astronaut," I said in a serious voice. "My name is Frances Star. My pee floats."

He yanked the helmet off, and my hair cracked with static. I wanted to grab his lacrosse stick and pretend it was a double-edged sword, but he kissed me. The helmet, along with my fantasies of greatness, rolled under his bed.

I'm a lacrosse player, I imagined saying to Susan. *I have a penis. Let me drape my letterman jacket over your shoulders. Let me unzip your spine.*

I'm a movie star's daughter, I imagined next. *Let me take you into the greenroom, whatever that is. Let me take you to the top of a sparkling mountain. Let me take you underneath the hot lights. They will photograph us kissing and make a billboard out of it. Which do you like better?*

I imagined myself in both places and wondered if my choice to stay or go would affect my spleen or my pancreas. I wanted to put the helmet back on.

In kindergarten, when the teacher asked us what we wanted to be when we grew up, I said, "A falcon." I wanted to fly, to beat gravity, so that it didn't own me.

What is my thing? I wondered. It had to be somewhere inside me, hidden like the room behind Lincoln's head at Mount Rushmore.

"You're beautiful," said Brad, as if answering my thoughts.

Then he kissed the spot where my beak would have been if I were a falcon.

I knew he was too worried about a repeat of what happened at Scottie's party to try and actually have sex with me now, but I also knew it was coming.

Maybe Brad wouldn't be the worst person to do it with. I just hoped he didn't try to light *candles* or anything like that. I didn't think I could handle it if he tried to light candles.

The Groupies

A group of us went to the movies, to see Johnny Moon in his new role as Grigori Rasputin in *Mad Monk*. Since he filmed a movie here, people sort of took ownership of him and followed what he did, which was mostly romantic comedies and horror movies. This was his first big "serious role."

The trailer had been playing over and over for weeks on the television in our kitchen. Sandra usually left the room when it came on.

It was opening night, and the theater was full. I couldn't tell if it was just in my head, but I felt people's eyes on me.

I sat somewhere near the middle with a box of Sno-Caps, between Susan and Brad. During the trivia, when the lights dimmed, Brad reached over and took my hand. I saw Susan watching. In response, almost like a reflex, she linked her arm through mine, on my other side, and rested her head on my shoulder.

"Who's Rasputin again?" Susan whispered in my ear.

"A Russian guy," I whispered back.

After I saw the trailer for the first time, I looked Rasputin up on the internet. He started as a peasant, then became a powerful mystic, close to the royal family. When I imagined meeting Johnny Moon, I wondered if my life would be anything like Rasputin's rise to fame—you know, without the whole being-murdered thing.

"Yeah, but what did he *do*?" Susan whispered back.

"He healed people," I said. "He was magical."

The lights dimmed. Heather and Scottie were already making out. An old couple next to us glared at them, and for a moment, I felt a warm feeling of belonging. This was why being popular was good—it was nice to be part of the group that people glared at for making out in public, for being too loud, for having too much fun.

"It's cold in here," Susan whispered, burying her head further into my neck. My stomach clenched, and I felt warm all over.

Then Johnny Moon's face appeared on the screen.

Sometimes it felt like nothing in my life was actually mine except for him.

He was really too young for the role, but they needed someone handsome, someone whose face was recognizable enough to impress the public with their makeup work, and to conjure sympathy in the average viewer. The long beard he wore in the film completely disguised his elegant features, and I cried when he healed Alexei Romanov.

Susan fell asleep before the movie was half-over—I felt her warm, steady breath on my skin. It smelled like cheap, plasticky chocolate. I wanted her to stay there forever.

I glanced at Brad, who was rapt by the movie. In the low light of the screen, his eyelashes made shadows on his cheeks. He was beautiful too. I was surrounded by beautiful people. On either side, their legs touched mine.

I looked back at the screen.

Most of the world thinks that Rasputin was assassinated for political reasons, but the details aren't clear, which I learned when I looked him up. Historians and other people who study political things have different theories. Just like both Johnny Moon and me, Rasputin had a bunch of groupies. I knew that Bridget Murphy, the head of the wannabe group, and her friends were staring at me *right now*. Rasputin supposedly had sex with lots and lots of teenagers and charged tons of money to heal people. They paid. Many people believed that the reason it took so many tries to kill him was that he really did have healing power, and others thought he was an evil alien.

In the movie, Johnny Moon was shown in Siberia, exiting a church, when a prostitute, a disciple of the monk Iliodor, stabbed him and then shouted, "I have killed the Antichrist!"

Johnny Moon recovered from that, but after the stabbing, he became addicted to opiates. Later on in the film, he was poisoned, beaten, and shot four times, then drowned in a partially frozen river.

I knew this was Hollywood—maybe history was different. Hollywood didn't bother with autopsies. It only cared about drama.

I couldn't help but imagine myself with him. With a dad.

During the closing scene, Brad leaned over and whispered in my ear, "You look like him, a little. You guys have the same nose."

In my dreams that night, and for many nights after, I saw Johnny Moon's bloodied face and cold, still, fishlike eyes, his bluish body buoyant in the water, surrounded by jagged floating chunks of ice. I woke up with my hands shaking, sweat gathering on the base of my back.

The Plan

The last time I had nightmares, like the ones I'd just started having about Johnny Moon frozen in the river, happened in seventh grade, after Corvis handed me the note.

Do you think about girls the way Susan thinks about Brad? — C

I'd been carrying the note since she gave it to me, trying to figure out what to do with it. The night before, I dreamed that Corvis took my hand and led me to a Victorian castle full of girls, all beautiful, all with long braided hair. I woke sweating, with my hand in my underwear, and I knew I had to do something about it.

The next day, I gathered Susan and Heather in the middle school cafeteria, which smelled like dish soap and french fries.

"Come on," I said, watching Corvis move forward in the line for sloppy joes. After she got her lunch, she was supposed to join us. She tapped her foot nervously, the sole of her Adidas sneaker jiggling.

We vacated our reserved table. Brad and Scottie and a couple of other boys from the lacrosse team were still sitting there—we were the only girls who sat with boys at lunch in seventh grade.

The rest of the cafeteria was separated by both gender and

social status. Sitting with boys showed that we were mature.

The other tables were full of kids just a little bit less pretty, a little bit more gangly, a little more wide-eyed. At one table, everyone wore black and had faces full of acne scars. We called them the Death Brigade. Kristen Duffy was one of them. At another table, there were girls who looked like us from far away, but up close you could see physical flaws that their Abercrombie clothes couldn't hide. A flat butt, a huge nose, limp hair, or a pear-shaped body. PJ Greenberg sat with them sometimes, but she was trying to move toward sitting with us.

The note was still in my pocket, as heavy as a rock.

When we got inside the closest girls' bathroom, I shooed out Bridget Murphy—a leading member of PJ Greenberg's group— who was using a pocket sewing kit to fix a button that had ripped from her shirt.

I grabbed the hall pass Bridget had set on the sink and pushed it into her chest. It was a piece of wood shaped like an atom, which meant she had science.

"Go," I said, not calling her by name, even though we'd all been in school together since kindergarten.

Bridget looked at me, fear in her eyes.

"I need to fix this," she said, holding the fabric of her shirt between two fingers. "You can see my bra."

"We need to be alone," I said, pushing the hall pass deeper into her chest. "There are thirty million other bathrooms."

Bridget stared at us.

"*Go*," said Heather. "This is secret."

Bridget grabbed the hall pass, holding it over her exposed chest, and fled.

"Okay," I said, backing against the door, holding it shut. "Listen."

"What is it?" Susan asked. I could tell she was getting worried.

"It's Corvis," I said.

"What about her?" Heather leaned against the wall, one hand on her hip.

"She's a *lesbo*," I said, trying to sound scandalized.

"*What?*" Susan's eyes widened.

"Yep," I said. "A real live dyke."

Heather raised her eyebrows. Getting—and keeping—Heather's interest was a delicious feeling.

I pulled the note out, and read it to them in a dramatic voice.

"See?" I said.

"Well," said Heather, "we have to destroy her." Her voice was matter-of-fact.

"How do you know she's serious?" Susan asked.

"Have you seen her sneakers?" Heather countered. "Lesbo sneakers. One hundred percent."

Heather's reaction was proof of how easy it was to fall off the edge of the popularity cliff. You could lose everything in a second.

"Sleepover tomorrow night," I said. "My house."

Heather nodded, sealing it.

"We have to do this quick and dirty," she said. "Expose her."

I looked at Susan.

"You in?" I asked.

Susan shifted her weight from one leg to the other. She sighed.

"Fine," she said. "Okay."

"Give me that note," Heather said to me. "I'll keep it safe."

I held it to my chest. I wanted to keep it. I wanted to read it over and over again before the sleepover, to hold on to the feeling of being understood, until we ruined it.

"No way," I said.

"Don't lose it," Heather warned.

"Can I go eat my lunch now?" Susan asked.

Heather and I both shot her the same look of disapproval. Caring about eating was not cool.

"Just be there tomorrow night," I said to Susan. "Seven o'clock. Bring your camera."

Walking back to the cafeteria, I felt both alive and incredibly guilty. And I wondered how many people had caught a glimpse of Bridget Murphy's bra.

The Two Worlds

Do you really think I look like Johnny Moon?" I asked Brad the day after we saw *Mad Monk*.

We sat on his living room sofa, wrapped in a Pendleton blanket. His kindness annoyed me, but I tried to push that away. I looked for things to like about him instead.

For one thing, he loved his dog so much that it was heartbreaking. This dog, a wire-haired thing he found in a dumpster in Cohasset, was named Stinky Lewis. Brad taught him how to roll over, and they were both proud.

I would have pinned Brad as the golden retriever type, but I was wrong.

Another thing was, Brad kind of understood me. At least, he knew what it was like to be expected to feel lucky that you're pretty. Also, the way he touched my hand so carefully gave me the impression that he knew I didn't really want him, and maybe even why.

Stinky Lewis jumped into my lap, and I curled my fingers in his wiry fur.

As it turned out, Brad and I didn't have sex right away. There was some groping and kissing, sometimes he touched my boobs, but then I would laugh, and instead of going further we would take a walk or watch a movie, or play with Stinky Lewis.

The dog spent a lot of his time running around inside Brad's house, wagging his tail hopefully. The O'Hallorans had a fenced-in backyard, where Stinky Lewis also liked to go, running around in circles and eating his own poop.

He jumped from the couch now and did a few laps.

It was raining. We watched Stinky Lewis run back and forth between the front door and the back door, and I said, "I wonder if he thinks the doors lead to two different worlds."

Brad rubbed his feet together. He wore striped wool socks and suede house shoes.

"Yeah," said Brad. "He's like, hey—it's raining in Walking World, but let's check Poop-Eating World!"

Stinky Lewis did another lap from the living room to the kitchen. He barked and raised his ears, eager.

"He wants out," said Brad. He stood to open the back door, and Stinky Lewis wiggled everywhere, spinning in circles, until he saw the rain. Then he whined and sat down on the kitchen floor.

"Sorry, buddy," said Brad, sitting beside me again. "It's raining in both worlds today."

Honestly, what hurt the most was that he was nice. And Susan was nice. And they probably belonged together. Being Brad's girlfriend built a wall between them and gave me power that I knew was probably temporary, but imagining them together still hurt.

Thinking of Susan and her niceness, and how it matched with Brad and his niceness, made me say, "Want to go up to your room and fuck?"

Brad looked surprised.

I tugged at the blanket, and he stood. I wanted so badly to be normal, and I thought maybe this would help. I led him up the staircase, the walls lined with photographs of Brad's smiling family over the years, wearing matching navy-and-white sweaters and khakis, mostly taken at the Sears photo center. Their faces were genuine, hopeful. I felt like they were asking me to join them.

We reached his bedroom, and the air was charged.

This was it.

I let him take off my clothes and run his hands all over me, and then I closed my eyes. I could feel everything happening: The pain of him entering me, the warm blood coming out of my body. The noises Brad made that seemed different from any noises I would make—if I were to make any while this was happening.

I stayed silent, kind of held my breath, and told myself that sex was going to make me normal.

To help with not concentrating on the pain, I pictured Johnny Moon inviting Susan and me into his mansion, then I imagined him as Rasputin, marrying us in front of an altar of yellow roses.

When Brad finished, I let him keep his arm around me. I closed my eyes and concentrated on whether or not I felt different. I couldn't tell.

I reached for his bedside table and turned on the radio. A female announcer with a British accent was reporting on the EgyptAir flight that had crashed off the coast of Massachusetts a few weeks ago, killing all 217 passengers on board.

"They never made it to Egypt," I said. I thought of the plane going down, the lights flickering, the screaming. I wondered if the people on the plane held each other's hands while it was happening, even if they were strangers.

Brad was sweating. I tried to pretend it didn't gross me out.

"Can you even imagine Egypt?" he asked. "I mean, what it's really like, not how it looks in textbooks."

"No," I said. "For all I know, Egypt is fake."

"Asia too," he said.

"Don't you want to go places?" I asked. Listening to the radio, even though that particular plane went down—maybe *because* it went down—gave me the urge to go on a plane for the first time. It sounded exciting and dangerous.

"Yeah," Brad said, "I love Hopuonk, but sometimes I imagine going away."

"Why don't we ever go anywhere?" I asked. I imagined myself as a pilot, even though I wasn't smart enough to be one.

"I guess I'm scared," he admitted. "I mean, what if I like somewhere else so much that I decide to stay and not take over my dad's business?"

"So what?" I said. But I knew what he meant. It was like we'd made a promise to our parents and our grandparents, to everyone who came before us, that unless we were going to run off and cure cancer, we would stay here and keep Hopuonk going.

I thought of the beautiful cedar houses lining the edge of Humming Rock Beach, and how I didn't know a single person who owned one. The best properties in town belonged to the leaf peepers—those smiling, shiny-haired, crisply dressed people from Boston and New York who came to watch the leaves turn in fall, or to sunbathe on the beach in the summer. We collected their money for beach parking, but mostly, we didn't notice them and they didn't notice us.

Brad shrugged.

"It feels like everything is already decided," he said.

"Is it?"

"It feels that way," he said. "My dad's already started training me to take over. It's like I was born to be a landscaper."

"Do you like it?"

"You know, I actually do. I'm a really good landscaper," he said. His voice was hard.

I stayed silent, letting him finish.

"Sometimes," he said, "the fact that I'm so good at it really pisses me off."

I sat up and pulled on my shirt, leaving my bra on the floor.

He looked at me.

"What is it that makes me so good at it?" he asked. "I mean, is it because I've been watching my dad all these years, or is it, like, in my actual blood?"

I got what he meant.

"I think about that all the time," I admitted. "Like, is it our bodies that make us stay, that hold us back, or is it just that we're obedient?"

I didn't want to be obedient.

His eyes changed, like he'd just realized that we'd done it, that we'd had sex. He reached for my shirt and slid it back off.

"I want to make you feel good," he said. I couldn't look at his naked body.

Gently, but still abruptly, he disappeared under the covers and started going down on me again. This was the first time since the Datsun and the herpes.

I thought of Susan—her wet-laundry smell, her salty-girl smell, her smell that matched the air in Hopuonk, her arm in mine, her laugh like a champagne glass shattering on tile, the sweaty curls escaping from her bun after ballet practice, her neatly tucked spine, her battered feet, her Herbal Essences shampoo, her Stradivarius-shaped body, the nip of her nose, her tiny, silver-dollar-sized nipples—and I went away.

My body pulsed, and I came. Ashamed, I returned to where I really was, on Brad's Eddie Bauer sheets.

What should my next mistake be? I wondered.

"Taylor?"

There was Brad's face, his lips moist with me. I shuddered all over again but tried to pretend it was out of pleasure.

Don't say it, I thought.

"Taylor?" he said again.

"What?"

"Are you okay?" he asked.

The Same Pajamas

The night of the sleepover we'd arranged to destroy Corvis, we sat in the middle of my bedroom in a circle, playing with Corvis's Ouija board. My stomach knotted up, thinking of what I was about to do.

Corvis lived in a beautiful old Victorian, not quite as old as Susan's house, but nicer. It was painted in actual Victorian colors, bright fuchsia and turquoise, ornamented with gingerbreading.

We were all pretending everything was normal, waiting for the right moment to out her.

I kind of liked the Ouija board, but Susan said it was creepy and weird after Corvis wouldn't let her ask the spirits if Brad liked her. Heather said it was embarrassing. We were right in the middle of establishing contact with Kurt Cobain when Heather interrupted.

"This is gay. Kurt Cobain was just a grungy loser anyway."

Susan shifted uncomfortably.

"I'm scared," she admitted.

"Susan's scared," Heather said, looking at me rather than at Corvis.

"Maybe we should stop," I said to Corvis, taking my fingers off the planchette, though I wanted Susan to be scared so she would ask me to share her sleeping bag. I felt like Corvis knew this, and had brought the Ouija board for this reason.

At every sleepover, my pajamas and Corvis's were most alike. Long-sleeved. Plaid.

After that night, I started wearing nightgowns.

"You don't believe in ghosts, do you?" Corvis asked Susan, smirking.

"No," Susan said uncertainly. She was wearing Laura Ashley floral pajamas: a matching tank top and shorts, with lace on the edges and at the neckline.

"Do you believe in God?" Corvis asked, her eyes narrowing.

"Of course I do," Susan said in a small voice.

"Well, he's basically just a ghost," said Corvis. "In churches, they even call him one."

Heather, who was Catholic, said, "You're so weird, Corvis."

Heather's mind was made up about Corvis the second she saw the note. Heather had always competed with Corvis—I think because Corvis never seemed insecure—and this was her chance to win.

Heather looked at me.

"Remind me," she said, "why did you start inviting her to sleepovers?"

To see if her pajamas were like my pajamas.

"Shut up, Heather," I said. Heather wore a nightgown with bunnies on it. Also, the collar was lace.

"You're probably going to grow up to be Wiccan," she said to Corvis. "Aren't you?"

Corvis looked surprised. She was the last member to join our group, but she'd been accepted so long ago that she wasn't used to Heather treating her this way.

"I'm Catholic," Susan said.

"It's stupid to try and guess what's going to happen," said Corvis, who wasn't anything.

I wasn't Catholic either. My problems were accumulating. Corvis and I had the same kind of pajamas, and we were both heathens. I had to go through with the plan.

"Think about Kurt Cobain's daughter," I said, to change the subject. "Like, he's her *dad*."

"I know," Susan said. "And her middle name is Bean." She shuddered.

"He's not her dad anymore," Heather said.

"Of course he is," said Corvis. "When someone dies, it doesn't mean they're not still your dad." She looked at me. "Or if they leave."

"Taylor doesn't have a dad," Heather said.

"Yes," said Corvis, "she does."

"Well then," said Heather, "where is he?"

I stiffened. I didn't like when other people talked about my missing father. "I don't know," I said.

Heather crossed her arms over her chest.

"We could try to find him," said Heather, gesturing to the Ouija board.

"No," I said.

"That's what I thought," Heather said, looking at me with a satisfied expression on her face.

We'd somehow gotten away from our plan.

"I know what to ask it," I said. "Let's ask it who *Corvis* loves."

Heather's eyes lit up again.

Susan looked nervously from Corvis to me, to Heather, and back to me.

"You're supposed to ask the spirits questions you can't answer in real life," Corvis said. "If you wanted to know who I love, you could just ask me."

"Fine," said Heather. "Who do you love, Corvis?"

"No one," said Corvis.

"Liar," said Heather.

I pulled the note from my pocket, unfolded it, and held it up. Corvis's eyes widened.

"You weren't supposed to show that to anyone," she said to me.

Game time. Adrenaline kept me going.

"It's Taylor," Heather said. "Isn't it? She's who you love."

This shocked me. I hadn't considered this as part of Corvis's gayness, and I found it sort of strange that Heather had jumped to that conclusion.

Corvis said nothing. She looked about seven times smaller.

"Prove it," said Heather. "Prove you don't want to kiss Taylor."

Susan hugged her legs to her chest.

"Do it," I said. "Kiss me. Then we can tell if it's real or fake."

"No way," said Corvis.

I leaned back, my pajama top slipping off my shoulder.

"I know you want to," I said, struggling to maintain a confident tone for Heather. "Prove me wrong."

Corvis rolled her eyes.

"Fine," she said.

She crawled toward me on all fours and leaned in. This was one of the slowest seconds of my life—I had enough time to smell the scent of pine on her, a nice smell, like she used her father's deodorant or something. I had enough time to register that her lips were chapped, that she'd just brushed her teeth, that her hair was coarse and prickly. I remember everything about that moment—I would remember it even without the photograph that circled the school the following Monday, making the event visible and permanent.

Heather pulled out Susan's Polaroid and snapped the photograph. It showed Corvis leaning toward me, and me leaning back— evidence that I didn't initiate.

Corvis instantly pulled away when she heard the click of the camera.

Though I recognized our sameness in the kiss, I also knew that Corvis didn't want to kiss me. It was true that she wanted girls, but I was not one of them.

If everyone had looked closely at the photograph, they would have seen that Corvis didn't mean it, but no one looked closely. No one looked closely when Heather and I made copies of both the photograph and Corvis's note and tossed them everywhere around school.

"What are you doing?" Corvis demanded.

Heather held up the photograph.

"You're disgusting," she said. *"Lesbian."*

Corvis turned to me. I raised my eyebrows.

"Don't try to deny it," I said. "Just go home."

The following week, after the picture circulated, everyone kept coming up and asking me if I was okay. As if she had poisoned me.

The Pirates

After Brad and I had sex, I wasn't sure when I was supposed to do it again, or how often. To dodge it one night, I suggested we steal Scottie's father's boat instead.

"Can I take you on an actual date?" Brad asked on the phone, and I said, "Yes, let's go steal a boat and find some gold."

Even though Susan and I had shopped for my date outfit with Brad back at Halloween time, we'd never actually done anything but hang out at each other's houses.

I knew he was thinking dinner at O'Reilly's as an actual date, but I hadn't been into dinner lately. I'd been into cigarettes, whiskey in the bathtub, and Dr Pepper–flavored ChapStick.

When he picked me up wearing an ironed button-down and khakis, I felt defeated. He looked too eager, and I felt a constant nagging inside me that I was disappointing him—almost the same way I felt about Sandra. I wore a pair of ripped corduroys and one of Sandra's lover's old Patriots sweatshirts with thumb holes, and zero makeup, except for the Dr Pepper ChapStick.

"Okay," I said, trying to get into the mood, "put on your best pirate face."

"Are you sure about this?" he asked. "I can still take you to dinner. Lobster, even, if you want."

Lobster would definitely make me puke, especially if it was followed by sex, especially if the sex was followed by cuddling.

"I'm sure," I said. I got into his car, saw his lacrosse helmet in the back seat, and pulled it over my head.

We drove to the pier, and when we got out of his Datsun, we were greeted by November's hateful winds. I stared out at the ocean. Tonight, it was black, reflecting only the pale moon and the small lights of boats.

"You know I'm allowed to borrow the boat whenever," said Brad, "but it's choppy out right now."

"I love choppy," I said, adjusting the helmet.

I started down the dock, and reached for the rope, struggling to untie it.

Brad stopped me and undid the knots in two seconds. I was jealous of him for making it look so easy.

I climbed on board, and he followed. The night was felty and close to our faces. The smell of salt was overpowering, and the waves crashed angrily against the shore. I stood at the wheel of the boat, ready to steer us to some imagined island. It would be named Infinity Island, and it would be inhabited by barefoot women with purple skin and many bracelets, who ate things like ostrich eggs and drank the blood of cats.

But when Brad tried to start the engine, it puttered and stopped.

We found ourselves in the cabin, freezing, and I had the startling realization that this was where Brad had lost his virginity to Heather.

I think Brad realized the same thing.

"What was it like, when you and Heather did it here?"

Brad looked embarrassed.

"Why would you ask me that?" he said. "It was a long time ago, and now I'm here with you."

I remembered Heather telling me about it, how she used advice from *Cosmo*. It was an article called "11 Reasons to Swallow," and she'd explained it to me at work, why boys found it rude when you didn't swallow after you gave them a blow job, like it was a rejection. She also said another article suggested covering their bodies in whipped cream, but she'd tried it and said it got sticky and, overall, was terrible advice. I wanted to know if Brad liked being with Heather and if she liked being with him. Also, I wondered if I was bad at sex, if Heather was better than me.

"I just wondered," I said, shrugging. "Did she seem happy?"

"Let's just be here together," he said, "and not talk about anyone else."

He closed the door behind us, dulling the crash of the waves. As we shivered, as our teeth clattered together, sounding like broken windup toys, he leaned into me. He slid his hand under my shirt, his icy skin touching my back. I thought again of the whipped cream and wondered if *Cosmo* was full of shit. But then again, it *did* teach me to get myself off with the showerhead.

He wanted to kiss me. He reached for the helmet, trying to pull it over my head, but I shoved his arm away.

"This stays on," I said.

"What is it with you and my helmet?" he asked, picking me up by the waist and setting me down, like a glass of wine or a school art project or a porcelain doll, on the small bed. The helmet bumped against the frame, and I blinked at his face, dizzy.

"I just like the way it feels," I said.

It hid me inside myself, where no one could get. It also made me feel powerful, like I could fly planes or beat up a Viking. Girls never got to wear helmets. We had to wear heels. We had to wear thongs.

My question was answered. We would do it regularly, and it would become normal. We would do it on beds, but also in cars and on boats. We would do it in the sand, on the forest floor, and again and again on his Eddie Bauer sheets. Brad had condoms in his wallet, and I knew in that moment that the unwrapping of one, the hospital smell of the latex, would become part of my life now.

Again as he entered me, again as it hurt, I went away.

The boat rocked back and forth in the current, and I imagined myself with Susan, pretending our childhood beds were pirate ships.

Let's go find some gold.

I always knew there was no gold in Hopuonk—at least, not buried in the ground. I closed my eyes behind the helmet, and

Brad's heavy breathing reminded me why I'd wanted to search for gold so much as a kid.

If you had gold, you could buy a ship, or a plane. You could escape.

I should have just eaten the lobster.

The Party

Just like every year, we ate Thanksgiving dinner at Susan's house. Her parents thought it was sad that there were only two of us in our family. Unlike us, they had a dining room, with a big antique table they only used on special occasions, and china to match. Susan's mother sat with an ashtray in front of her, a cigarette in one hand and a glass of wine in the other, ignoring her plate. Susan's father's plate was piled high with turkey, stuffing, and mashed potatoes, gravy seeping around the edges. I thought of the marks on Susan's back and wanted to shove his plate into his face and smash his nose in.

Susan and I both had small portions—me, because turkey grossed me out, the stringiness of it, the bones showing, and her because she was always trying to lose weight.

"Tell us how things are going with Brad," Mrs. Blackford probed, taking a long drag of her cigarette. Her tone was somewhat accusatory, like I didn't deserve him as a boyfriend.

"They're doing well," Sandra answered for me, taking a small bite of green bean casserole. Sandra wasn't a big eater. She picked at things, then set them down. "He had flowers delivered to the house out of the blue," she added proudly.

Susan sighed theatrically.

"You're so lucky," she said to me, which put me in a bad mood.

I looked around the room—at the photographs on the far wall of Susan with her parents over the years in the Sears photo room, at her school photographs collecting dust in their wooden frames. Even in the early nineties, when the backgrounds you could choose from were awful—neon stripes or fake trees—Susan never went through an awkward stage. She always looked perfect. I shuddered, because none of the pictures showed the welts on her back where her father hit her with his belt, nor did they show her mother sitting at the kitchen table, smoking two cigarettes at once. Then I looked at everyone's plates, and it grossed me out how full they were. There were only five of us.

"You know, this holiday is pretty messed up," I said, trying to change the subject. We took field trips to Plimouth Plantation every year in primary school, where you could visit Pilgrim houses and Wampanoag huts, each side separate. On the Pilgrim side, everyone was an actor, staying in character no matter what, with fake-sounding British accents. On the Wampanoag side, everything was serious, and the people who populated the scene were the only actual Wampanoags I've ever seen. "They act like everyone got along so well, like the dinner was some giant awesome party, when, really, everything was terrible."

"Don't be negative," Sandra said mildly, not looking at me. Then, with her eyes on Susan's father, she said, "The flowers were really beautiful."

"You should get flowers for *me* more often," said Susan's mom, also looking at her husband. Other than at Thanksgiving, they were almost never together.

I saw Sandra exchange a knowing glance with Mr. Blackford, like they were in on some kind of joke together.

"Brad is the cutest boy in our whole school," Susan said. "He has been since primary." That prompted me to remember Thanksgiving back then, when they had half of us dress as Pilgrims for school the day before break, and half of us as Indians. We fought over the Indian costumes, with their feathered hats made out of construction paper, their fringed pants, which we loved in comparison to the white smocks and white triangular hats the Pilgrims wore.

"Seriously," I said, getting annoyed at everyone at the table for discussing my life when I didn't feel like it. "The Pilgrims killed the Indians, and gave them smallpox, and then made the rest of them move away. Everything here is named after them, but I've never even met one at the grocery store. They never tell us the whole story. They act like it was just a great party all the time."

I was aware that I was talking about myself, that I was also sick of everyone thinking my life was one big awesome party, but no one else seemed to notice.

Susan's mom lit another cigarette, which she brandished at us. "Eat your food, girls," she said, her own fork untouched beside her plate. "There are kids starving in India."

This argument never made sense to me.

"Just mail my plate to them, then," I said. "Better yet, mail it to the nearest Indian reservation, with an apology note."

Susan's mom glared at me, but Sandra said, "Don't force her to eat."

I brought my fork to my mouth, accidentally dropping a green bean on the floor. When I reached down to pick it up, I saw Sandra's foot touching Mr. Blackford's under the table. I blinked, and Sandra's foot quickly moved back under her chair, like it had been there all along.

"Are you and Brad going to match your clothes at prom?" Susan asked me, flipping the hair out of her eyes.

"Prom isn't until April," I said. "I have no idea."

"You should match," she said firmly. "Make him get a tie the same color as your dress."

I glanced at Sandra, who looked kind of guilty. Surely, it wasn't because we killed the Indians.

"This holiday is so racist," I said, taking a bite out of a dinner roll. I realized I sounded like Corvis.

I thought about having sex with Brad in Scottie's father's boat, and prayed they would change the subject. I couldn't bear to tell them how wrong it felt, how badly I didn't want to end up like Susan's parents.

And I still wanted to ask Corvis about scissoring.

The Hall Pass

It was the first week of December when Corvis got her acceptance letter from Sarah Lawrence College. I was sitting in Mr. Sheehan's Algebra II class, next to Susan and Heather, when I heard whispers about it. Corvis wasn't there, because she didn't take algebra. She took calculus, obviously.

None of us in Mr. Sheehan's class got early decision letters—we were headed to trade school. Or maybe we would just have a baby and get married and live in our parents' basements.

I started to imagine it, Sarah Lawrence. It would be beautiful, with stone buildings and professors wearing tortoiseshell eyeglasses and tweed. There would be classrooms where students sat in circles and said what they thought—about the death penalty and abortion and President Clinton, subjects we weren't supposed to discuss at Hopuonk High—and other things too. Things I didn't even know existed, like the opinions of French philosophers. I bet they even had opinions about the opinions of French philosophers.

Corvis had a Darwin fish decal on her car, a statement against the Jesus fish everyone else had. I didn't know what it stood for, so I looked it up on the internet. I learned that the Jesus fish was called the *ichthys*, and that the fish with legs was a parody of that. Corvis was arguing against evolutionary creationism with her car. Probably Sarah Lawrence was full of kids with parody bumper stickers, and all of it made me feel stupid, because I had to look everything up on the internet just to figure out what my opinion was.

The only bumper sticker on my Volvo was a little purple circle that said KISS 108 FM, BOSTON'S #1 HIT MUSIC STATION. It was free, and everyone else had it too.

At Sarah Lawrence, they probably dyed their hair pink and purple, and pierced things, and their tattoos would be quotes from Shakespeare plays. They would lean back in their seats and exhale deeply before they spoke, and their conversations would have nothing to do with boobs, or highlights, or homecoming crowns.

I didn't like reading, or school—at least not Hopuonk High. I didn't want to take philosophy or sociology classes, but I desperately wanted to exist in a different kind of social space. Massachusetts College of Pharmacy and Health Sciences would probably be another version of Hopuonk High—except I'd have to take even harder, more boring classes.

"Taylor?" Susan poked me in the ribs with her pencil.

"What?" I shout-whispered. When I looked over, I saw Heather looking at me, too, her eyes heavily rimmed in black eyeliner.

"Are you going to Scottie's party tonight?" Susan asked. It seemed like our lives revolved around parties at Scottie's house.

"If I'm alive," I said absently. Mr. Sheehan shot us a glance of warning and continued scribbling equations on the blackboard.

I was still failing algebra. My average was a 23 percent. I just didn't get it. I didn't care either.

I had sent in my application to Massachusetts College of Pharmacy and Health Sciences that morning. When I dropped the packet off at the post office, my stomach had sunk.

What was I doing? What was I going to do?

"I have to go to the bathroom," I said to Mr. Sheehan, who barely looked over at me. He'd already decided that I was an idiot, and he was basically right.

I grabbed the hall pass from his desk and shoved it under my armpit, because I hated touching it. Who knew where the hell that thing had been?

Instead of actually going to the bathroom, I kept walking. Straight out the back door to the student parking lot, past the parking lot monitor, who was doing a crossword puzzle. When I reached my rusted-out Volvo, I got inside and sat for a minute, trying to figure out where I was going. Then, I knew. Humming Rock Beach.

––––––––––

I threw the hall pass out the window at a red light and kept all the windows rolled down, even though it was freezing.

When I got to the seawall, Corvis was there.

"Hey," she said, acting unsurprised to see me. She was wearing an L.L.Bean fleece-lined flannel, and the tips of her pointy, elfish ears were bright red.

"I think I knew you'd be here," I said, sitting next to her. My coat was in my locker, and the wind went right through my cardigan.

She lit a cigarette and looked straight ahead at the ocean.

"Is Sarah Lawrence full of freaks and lesbians?" I asked.

"That's what I'm counting on," she said. She kind of smiled, but more at the ocean than at me.

"Why aren't you in calculus?"

Corvis shrugged. "I already got into college," she said, "so if I want to look at the ocean instead of going to class sometimes, I guess I can."

Corvis continued to look straight ahead, and we both watched a giant wave break against the sand.

"I think probably you need to leave," Corvis said. I wasn't sure if she meant leave the seawall or leave her alone, but then she said, "College isn't the only way."

A pair of horseshoe crabs stumbled across the beach, struggling over the rocks.

"It's easier for me," she said. "I know that."

"What do you mean?"

"I'm never in the *Mariner*," she said. "Nobody cares what I do or who I fuck. And I'm glad."

I looked at her sharply.

"I mean, sure, Scottie and the others call me names sometimes," she said, "but it's because they're bored. I'm not the kind of person they actually care about."

I pulled my knees to my chest, hugging myself.

Then she looked at me. Her barely-there eyebrows furrowed, and I could see in her face that someday, maybe in her thirties, she might be attractive, in an edgy sort of way. I felt certain that there was some woman in the world who would love her properly, and that she would have the ability to accept this love.

"You're beautiful," she said. It was not a compliment but a statement, almost like she was analyzing a piece of art. "There are places where that doesn't work against you."

"Whatever," I said. I reached for one of her cigarettes and lit it. A few moments passed, and then I said, "What kinds of places?"

Corvis shrugged again. She looked away, at the horseshoe crabs. One planted itself on top of a tangle of seaweed; the other was still moving toward the water. "You'll find them, if you want it enough."

"Corvis?"

"Yeah?"

"Why were you at the gynecologist that day?"

"Oh," Corvis said. "Well, I got a Ben Wa ball stuck in my vagina."

"A Ben Wa ball?"

"They're like these little balls that make your Kegel muscles—"

"No, I know," I said. "But . . . stuck?"

"Totally," she said.

I didn't know what to say. This was not the kind of thing that I would admit.

"I always pee when I laugh too hard," she said. "I thought they would help, but then . . ."

"What did you *say*?" I asked. "I mean, to the doctor."

"That I got a Ben Wa ball stuck up my vagina."

This completely shocked me. But then again, knowing Corvis, not really.

"What else would I say?"

I pictured her buying them, the balls, and I couldn't believe her bravery. We didn't have a sex shop, not in Hopuonk, not even anywhere but Boston. Did she go by herself? Did Kristen go with her for moral support? If so, did Kristen get them too?

I started laughing, thinking about Corvis going into the sex store and asking the person behind the desk for exactly what she wanted and explaining exactly why.

"Stop laughing!" she cried. "You're going to make me pee!"

Susan would never go to a sex shop with me, and I would never ask her to, even just to see what kinds of things they sold.

Suddenly, I had a realization: Susan wasn't funny. Not like Corvis.

I wouldn't have much more time with Corvis, to make it right, to be her friend again, to know her.

"We could do something crazy," I said. "You know, skip more than just math. Drive to Provincetown."

My voice sounded weak, like I was joking.

"I don't have bail money," Corvis said. "I don't even have tattoo money."

"What, are you scared?" I said.

Corvis shot me a look and stood, brushing the sand off the butt of her frayed blue jeans.

"Are you?" she asked.

And then she was gone. She left her calculus textbook behind on the seawall. She didn't need it anymore.

The Dairy Queen

On December 14th, Susan's dad had a heart attack while he was running on the treadmill in his basement.

It was a school night, and Brad was at my house when the phone rang, an unusual circumstance, because we usually hung out at his house or in his car. It was almost one o'clock in the morning, and we were sitting on the end of my bed, looking at Stephanie Tanner through the glass of her fish tank. I was getting ready to feed her while Brad rubbed a palm hopefully up and down my thigh.

"Come over," Susan said when I answered. Her voice was thick. "Now."

"What happened?" I asked.

"Come over," she said again. "My dad died." And then she hung up.

I held the phone next to my ear for almost a full minute. I wasn't crying, but I was definitely starting to hyperventilate.

"What?" Brad asked. "What happened?"

I dropped the phone slowly, letting it hang on the cord.

"Susan's dad died. I have to go."

Saying it out loud made it feel real. I didn't know anyone who died before, and it scared me. I decided I would walk so I could think about it on my way, so I could try to get rid of the relief I felt about the fact that he couldn't hit Susan anymore. I was pretty sure you weren't supposed to be glad someone was dead.

"Sorry," I said to Brad, putting on my peacoat. "I'll just see you later, okay?" I was still hyperventilating a little. My voice sounded stupid and small.

His face completely fell, and he grabbed my forearm as I reached for the knob on my bedroom door.

"Taylor?"

"What."

"Just . . ." He stopped. I could tell that this shocking news was pushing something out of him. Tears formed in the corners of his eyes, which made me feel bad, because I was nowhere near crying.

"*What?*" I demanded.

"I love you," he said. He reached out to touch my elbow, then changed his mind.

"Oh my God, Brad. *Not now.*"

I handed him Stephanie Tanner's fish food.

"Can you feed her, please?" I asked. Then I left him standing there in my bedroom.

I was nine when Sandra won Stephanie Tanner for me at the Hopuonk Fair. That night, after we got her a bowl, both of us crouched in front of the glass, watching her dart around.

"She's so cute," I said, staring at her glittering orange body. "It'll be so sad when she dies."

Which prompted Sandra to say, "You just *got* her, Taylor. How are you already this nostalgic? You're in fourth grade, for Christ's sake."

While walking to Susan's house, I started thinking about Mr. Blackford. He was a real asshole.

There was the time he pinned Mrs. Blackford against the kitchen wall and said, "Of course I'm fucking Mrs. Greenberg, because I don't get any at home," and Mrs. Blackford was crying.

She'd held her cigarette down real low, and I could tell she was thinking of squishing it right into his cheek.

Susan and I watched from the hallway. We were eleven. Mrs. Greenberg was PJ's mom. Her actual name was Debbie.

I remember thinking, *Don't you call people by their first names when you're sleeping with them?*

Susan was crying. She was holding my hand tight, and I hated both of her parents. At least when Sandra fucked people, she called them by their first names. Brian, Teddy, Frank. *Johnny*, I thought hopefully. They were people to her, at least.

Later that night, Mrs. Blackford brushed Susan's hair so hard that the hairbrush broke in her hair and pulled a chunk of it out.

Whenever her parents fought, they used Susan against each other. For example, once when Susan's mother said she couldn't eat sugar cereal, her dad bought her a family-sized box of Lucky

Charms, because he was angry. Susan ate Lucky Charms in a very specific way, by eating all the regular cereal pieces and leaving the marshmallows for the end, letting them turn the milk blue, which I knew because Sandra bought me sugar cereal whenever I wanted and Susan ate it at my house. But when Susan's mother saw her eating the Lucky Charms, she grabbed Susan by the elbow and threw her against the wall, then went to scream at Mr. Blackford.

Sometimes, like the night when they fought in the kitchen about Debbie Greenberg, they went straight for Susan, even if she didn't do anything wrong.

But then there was also the fact that Mr. Blackford would take us to Dairy Queen on Sunday nights and let us get whatever we wanted. Susan always got a butterscotch-dipped cone, and every time, I considered asking for a chili cheese dog, because it was the only non-dessert item on the menu, and I was curious. But instead, I always got an ice pop shaped like a star. And Mr. Blackford asked us about our week, and he actually seemed interested.

I could tell he wanted to remember being eleven, before everything got so bad. I understood his life a bit more now that I was older. He liked taking us for ice cream when we were kids because it reminded him of doing the same when he was young. Before he married a woman he did not love and got a boring job. Before he realized that even though he was the only one of his brothers to have a serious career, to go to college, it didn't make him happy. He had a long commute into Boston every day, and I bet he spent the whole trip honking at people.

The thing was, when somebody died, even if they were awful, you wanted to just remember them getting you anything you wanted at Dairy Queen.

———

Looking through the front window, I saw that Susan was wide-awake, wrapped in a quilt on her sofa, the low blue glow of the television illuminating her cheekbones, a bottle of Harpoon wedged in the crevice of her lap. Her long coal-colored hair was piled on top of her head in a bun.

I rapped lightly on the front door, and she looked over briefly before turning back to the television. I gently turned the doorknob and stepped inside.

Susan didn't look at me. She was watching the Discovery Channel, something with animals.

She usually watched *Entertainment Tonight*, soap operas, or sitcoms.

"I need a fennec fox," she said, her eyes never leaving the screen. "They're so sad. I can't handle it."

"Susan," I said. My stomach churned. I was afraid to approach her.

One of her bare feet stuck out from the quilt. Her toenails were painted a light shade of purple, even though she usually didn't bother with her feet because they were already messed-up.

She always took such good care of the rest of her body: her eyebrows, her cuticles. She had drawers full of creams and lotions and nail polish that she ordered from the ads at the back of *Cosmo*, concoctions to make her hair thicker, her lips shinier, her skin softer.

I expected Susan's house to be full of people delivering casseroles, then realized maybe that was coming later. Instead, there was just her mother in the kitchen, smoking a cigarette and staring at the wall, another cigarette going in the ashtray on the table.

"Maybe if I move to the Sahara," said Susan, "then I could get one. I would be willing to do that."

"I had to walk," I lied, moving a little bit closer. "My car wouldn't start." I slipped slowly out of my boat shoes, leaving them on the doormat.

"They only live for fourteen years," Susan said, finally turning to look at me. "I could move back to Hopuonk after it dies." Her cheeks and the tips of her ears were pink from the beer.

"Where is he?" I asked. This seemed like the stupidest question in the world, but it seemed impossible to me that he could be there, running, and then just not be.

Susan scooted over on the couch, making room for me, but not exactly inviting me to sit down. I gently squeezed into the space behind her, my stomach against her back.

"At the morgue, I guess," she said. She said "the morgue" as if it were the same as *the grocery store*. "My mom got back a little while ago."

Her voice was monotone. I guessed it was one of those things where you cry really, really hard and then you go numb. Then, probably, you cry again. I wondered if there was a part of her that felt relieved, that felt safer, knowing he couldn't hurt her anymore.

She took a sip of her beer, then sighed and leaned against me. On the television screen, two little almost-rodents with gigantic ears flitted through some desert brush.

"Their ears, like, keep out the heat," she said. "From their bodies. So they don't get too hot."

I wrapped my arms around her and hugged her as tightly as I could, pressing my cheek into her neck.

"I love you," I said. "I'm so sorry. I love you." I was crying now.

She grabbed one of my hands in both of hers and squeezed.

"Keep me warm?" she said, pressing my hand into her chest.

"Yes," I said.

In this moment, I felt strangely lucky. To be a girl, to be able to say these things and for them to be okay and normal to say. To tell the truth, even if it meant something completely different to me.

I also knew I didn't love Brad, that I never would, that I wouldn't be able to lie and tell him otherwise, and I knew I had to do something about it.

The Mistake

The following night, another school night, we threw a party to "make Susan feel better," which translated to us getting drunk together instead of letting Susan do it in her living room by herself, or with just me.

It was after closing at The Mooring. Scottie had the key, and we snuck in like we could get in trouble, as if Scottie's dad didn't know we were there, and as if the cops weren't all his buddies.

Scottie, one of the star lacrosse players, could pretty much do anything he wanted. I thought about that as I took my third shot of vodka—that maybe for him, the choice between comfort and life wasn't the same as it was for me.

Brad also seemed to have it easy. That is, until he told me he loved me. I hadn't told him I loved him back, or even acknowledged that he'd said it.

Mr. Blackford's death was a buffer. It allowed me an excuse to focus my attention on Susan, rather than on my growing dread about how to deal with Brad.

I slung my arm around Susan's waist and said, "See? Don't you feel a little bit better?"

Susan managed a nod. I handed her a shot.

The Mooring was dingy enough to keep the summer people and the leaf peepers out—this was our place. There were other bars and restaurants, like O'Reilly's, that charmed visitors, but not The Mooring. It was right across the street from Humming Rock, and the bar's sign didn't light up. Inside, it was dark, the paint was peeling, and the walls were decorated with dusty buoys, light-up Budweiser and Sam Adams signs, wooden steering wheels from old ships, and a taxidermy swordfish.

Heather kicked the jukebox, and Bob Dylan came on. "The Subterranean Homesick Blues." The music at The Mooring was old—Scottie's dad hadn't updated the jukebox in forever. The newest songs were probably Springsteen. Heather danced in the middle of the floor, and everyone joined in, including me.

PJ Greenberg, still in her stage makeup from the dress rehearsal of the community theater production of It's a Wonderful Life, turned on the microphone and belted out a song from her seat on top of the bar.

I pulled Susan along with me, spun her around. The vodka loosened her up, and when her hip crashed into mine, she actually let out a puff of laughter and took my hand.

"Get it, Susan!" PJ shouted.

Brad watched me. I felt his eyes on my back.

I danced my way behind the bar. It felt powerful there. I could see why Sandra liked it.

I handed out shots, swaying my hips with the music.

I thought about Sandra when she was my age. What did she think her life would be like? Her parents had both died the year she turned twenty-four and I turned three, in a car crash on the way home from a Red Sox game. Just like me, she had no siblings. Though it seemed to me that everyone loved her, she must have felt alone.

Brad was still watching.

Being behind the bar seemed better than standing over a stranger or, worse, someone I knew, cleaning their teeth. I had a feeling that I could end up like this—in charge of getting people wasted. I'd be much better at it than cleaning teeth, or popping out a couple of kids and driving them to soccer practice.

Scottie walked over, leaning so far over the bar that we almost touched.

"Give me a strong one," he said.

I reached for a bottle of Jim Beam, poured some into a shot glass, and set it in front of him.

I glanced at Susan, who was dancing with Heather and PJ, all of them in a tight circle. That was my favorite place to be, other than Susan's bed—in a small circle of girls, whispering, touching.

The song switched to "Red Red Wine" by UB40, a song I hated. I watched Susan shake her hips, her eyes closed. Her cheeks were flushed from the heat blasting in the bar, from dancing, from alcohol, from fear. She wouldn't stay this way forever. She wouldn't stay mine.

"Stay close to me. Don't let me be alone."

What horrible lyrics.

Scottie leaned in closer. His breath was sour, and I could see the tiny pores on his nose.

"Give me a little something," he said, jutting out his chin.

I leaned in, too, and pursed my lips. In a voice part Sandra, part Heather, I said, "You're disgusting."

"I'll take that as a compliment," said Scottie.

Brad watched. The girls watched, too, even while they danced. I felt Heather's eyes on me, waiting to see what I would do.

I put my cold hand on the back of Scottie's neck, making him jump a little. I pulled him in, bracing myself.

"You're a disgusting pig," I whispered. I felt the power that my body gave me. I could make Scottie react. I could use him.

Almost violently, I shoved my tongue down his throat. He kissed back, if you could even call it that. He wasn't gentle like Brad— he was bigger and more forceful. His tongue tasted like rubbing alcohol and cigarettes.

We were all animals.

I placed one hand firmly on each of Scottie's shoulders and shoved him away from me.

I could feel everyone's eyes on us now—but especially Brad's. This would have consequences, and I didn't know yet what they would be. Still, even if everyone hated me, I needed to do something to stop the current trajectory of my life.

"Come upstairs with me," Scottie pleaded. There was a small studio apartment there with a bed.

Everyone was still watching us, but the music was so loud they couldn't hear what we said.

"Never," I said, wiping his spit off my lips with the corner of my sweater. I grabbed the chest of his hoodie and yanked him toward me. I wanted to spit in his face. "You need to leave Corvis McClellan alone," I said.

He held his hands up in surrender, pouting like a five-year-old who'd just spilled orange juice on his mother's new white wall-to-wall.

There would be consequences for Scottie too. Brad was his best friend.

I walked over to the girls, took Susan by the arm, and led her out the door.

"Why did you do that?" Susan said as I pulled her toward my car. "Why did you kiss him?"

Sitting in my Volvo, gripping the steering wheel, with Susan in shotgun, I said, "Because I could."

———

When I was little, I didn't like it when Sandra sang. It was okay when she sang at open-mic night at The Mooring, where there was a microphone and it was expected, but when she sang by herself in the shower or the car, it was different.

For one thing, she would harmonize with cassette tapes, which

I believed she should have been embarrassed about. I didn't understand why she couldn't just sing along regularly, if she needed to sing along at all. Harmonizing required the kind of attention that caused her to drive recklessly, or burn dinner.

In the car, she played "Red Red Wine," which she had the cassette of, and sang it at the top of her lungs. That song was especially bad. When she sang, it was like I wasn't even there.

"Stop singing," I said to her once. I was six, sitting in the passenger seat, wearing a romper and a pair of jellies.

She kept singing, banging her palm on the steering wheel.

"Stop *singing*," I said again, louder. We were on our way to the Hanover Mall. I wanted a pair of clogs with wooden bottoms. Heather had them in every color. But Sandra said no, because I would trip and break my ankles.

That day we were going shopping for her only. She needed a pair of trousers. The clogs were never going to happen, even though I was sure I wouldn't break my ankles.

Again, I told her to stop singing.

"*No!*" she finally screamed.

When I covered my ears, Sandra said she couldn't enjoy it anymore.

"You're making me miss my favorite part," she said through her teeth.

I couldn't explain it, but it scared me—a song about being in love with wine.

Sandra pulled into the Webster Place strip mall parking lot—
the same strip mall where the plasma donation center and the
gynecologist were.

"Get out," she said.

I put my hands under my thighs. There were tears coming, hot
and itchy.

"No," I said in a little voice.

"Get *out!*" She reached across my lap and opened the passenger-
side door.

I got out. I guessed I'd made a big mistake, and I was bad. As she
drove away, the song blasted from the open window. I felt like I was
there for a really long time, but I guess it was only long enough for
her to go shopping for trousers.

While she was gone, I thought about hiding just to scare her for
leaving me there. But I didn't. I was sitting in exactly the same spot
when she came back. I wasn't crying anymore.

Back in the car, there was no music. The back seat was full of
Sears bags. I felt like a horrible person. Like I shouldn't have asked
for clogs.

While I waited for her to come back and get me, I imagined
her being voted homecoming queen in 1978, a year that I knew
basically nothing about. I pictured everyone with feathery haircuts
and ripped-up jeans. They lived in a dim-colored world, kind of
dreamy, and they looked a little bit like ghosts.

Sandra must have known she was going to win, but she acted like it was some giant surprise. Probably, she cried up there on the stage, held the microphone and thanked everyone profusely. She knew inside her heart that she only won for being beautiful and mean, and the power that came along with that.

When she was honest with herself, if she was ever honest with herself, I bet Sandra thought of that moment as the pinnacle of her life. I started to feel more and more guilty for asking her not to sing, especially because the pinnacle of her life had ended so long ago and she didn't have much to look forward to.

I wouldn't ask for clogs ever again. I decided that next time, even though I hated it, I would just let her sing.

The Crack

I spent the whole weekend at Susan's. When I got to school on Monday, I found out that Brad and I had broken up.

Susan spent her time at home drinking and watching *Full House*. The mom was dead on that show, but it felt far away, and they basically had three parents anyway.

We couldn't get Susan out of the house again. People did bring casseroles—they piled up in the fridge, then on the counter. I finally started tossing them, dish and all. Out of respect, I didn't eat much either. Susan's mom mostly stayed in the kitchen, saying, "You bastard," over and over again.

On Monday morning, I was in a stall in the girls' bathroom, trying to figure out whether or not my period had come and gotten on my skirt, when I heard PJ talking to Heather.

"Taylor Garland is a bitch. I can't believe she did that to Brad," said PJ. "Of course he would break up with her."

Break up? I tried to make myself as small and invisible as possible.

I lifted my feet, silently, from the floor and squatted on the toilet seat. I squinted through the crack in the stall door and saw that PJ, who had curly hair that I thought about sometimes, was in just her bra, washing something out of her shirt in the sink.

"I can't believe she did it to *you* either," PJ added.

Heather snorted.

"I'm not *with* Scottie," she said. "I don't care." She raised her eyebrows at PJ's reflection in the mirror. She looked a little bit relieved, even.

"Still," said PJ.

"Brad is so sweet," Heather said. She was reapplying foundation, frowning at her reflection and covering her freckles.

The word *bitch* stung a little, coming from PJ. She was my lab partner, and we were usually friends, but Heather had this way of looking at people that made them say cruel things. I knew because I'd been around Heather a lot, and it happened to me sometimes too. Heather was someone I wanted to conspire with, even if it felt terrible later. Heather was someone I wanted to impress, and someone I felt connected to by a magnetic force that I didn't quite understand.

"Yeah," PJ said, sighing dramatically. She liked Brad too. "I know."

Heather finished her makeup and looked again at PJ's reflection.

"Why do you *always* apply makeup like you're about to step out onstage?" she said. "Here, let me fix it."

PJ turned to Heather, and I watched Heather's hands moving a wet paper towel over PJ's cheeks, then applying foundation in a soft little circle. Heather had done this same thing to me many times, and it was just about the most intimate she ever was with another girl. I wanted to switch places with PJ—I wanted Heather's hands on my face.

"Thanks," said PJ, examining her new face. "You're so good at this."

Standing there, staring at PJ through the crack of the bathroom stall door, I couldn't help but think about her in primary school, of how we became friends.

In second grade, PJ peed her pants while wearing a semicolon costume in the grammar pageant. In front of everyone. She ran off the stage crying, and I ran after her. I was the question mark, the star of the show, even though I couldn't sing. PJ didn't get to sing her semicolon song, and the thing was, she actually *could* sing. It made you feel like crying when she sang. We collected gypsy moths during recess that day and put them in a shoe box, and I wouldn't let anyone make fun of her.

Now she was always the lead role in the school plays, and even though our theater department was terrible, she managed to save every play. Last year, during *Beauty and the Beast*, in the middle of a cardboard set that was falling down, she sang "Something There" so beautifully that you forgot Sonny O'Connell was even on the stage in that stupid gorilla costume.

"I can't believe Taylor, making out with Scottie *right* in front of Brad," said PJ. She was repeating herself now. "Aren't you pissed-off?"

"I think I'd be more pissed-off if I were Susan," Heather said absently.

Susan? I crouched lower. I didn't see how Susan factored into this. She didn't bring up Scottie all weekend. I guessed she was mostly glad to see me hurt Brad in public.

"I know. I mean, Susan is her best friend," PJ said. "And she always loved Brad, and Taylor is throwing it all away, right in front of her. Plus, her dad is dead."

I wondered if anyone knew Brad told me he loved me. I couldn't imagine him telling anyone, and I certainly hadn't.

"Susan is wicked annoying, but I still feel kind of bad for her," Heather said. "Her obsession with Brad has been *so* obvious since seventh grade."

"I know," PJ said, examining her shirt, now that her face was perfect. "Fuck. This salad dressing is *not* coming out."

I opened the stall door and walked through. "I have an extra shirt in my gym locker," I said casually.

PJ and Heather stared at me, their mouths open.

"Oh," PJ said. "No, that's okay."

Heather's face changed from shocked at being caught in the act of gossiping to a steady, calm look of superiority.

"Don't act surprised," she said to me, looking me straight in the eye. "You know all of this is true."

I ignored Heather, addressing PJ instead.

"Well, see you in biology," I said.

I left them there.

———————

I needed to find Brad. It was second period, so he had shop. I walked to the south wing of campus, then stood outside the shop classroom and waved to Brad, trying to stay out of Mr. Walsh's view.

When Brad saw me, he looked away, but I waved harder, and finally he went up to Mr. Walsh's desk and grabbed the hall pass, which was a little piece of metal shaped like a saw.

"So we're over?" I asked Brad when he got out into the hallway. "It's really awesome, hearing it from someone other than you."

I knew I had no right to be angry, but I was anyway. I was angry at him for making me feel guilty, for making me feel inadequate. I was angry at him for having been hurt by me.

"You tell me." His face was stony. He sounded like he had a cold.

"I don't know what to say," I said lamely. "Sometimes I just do stupid things for no reason."

But there was a reason, and we both knew it.

"You don't love me," he said to the floor. And then, in a smaller voice, "Scottie is my best friend."

"I'm sorry." I leaned against a puke-green locker. The words *Matt McDonough is a punk ass chump* were carved into the door.

"Are you sorry?" he asked. "Do you love me?"

I wished he hadn't asked me outright.

I pretended to think for a minute.

"No," I finally said.

Brad's eyes teared up, but I didn't feel like slapping him this time. I definitely didn't want to see him cry, but I also understood what you could expect from people.

"Just don't cry," I said anyway. It was more of an order than anything—I was trying to tell him how to act—how he was supposed to act. It was fine to be upset, but he shouldn't show it in public.

I thought about Mr. Blackford. How, probably, he should have just said that he didn't love Susan's mom. Then maybe Susan's mom could have found somebody else, and maybe she wouldn't be smoking two cigarettes at once in the kitchen all the time. And maybe Mr. Blackford wouldn't have had the chance to hurt Susan. Maybe he wouldn't have died.

"I knew it," Brad said. His voice sounded gray and chewed.

"Well," I said, "if it makes you feel any better, everyone hates me now."

Brad moved farther away from me. I watched him readjust his shoulders, setting them straight, standing tall. He looked better this way—angry, strong, clear-eyed. If he could only act that way more often, maybe I could have stayed with him.

"Everyone's always hated you," he said, in a tone not unlike Heather's when she was annoyed.

I felt like I was going to barf. I was definitely going to barf.

"I know," I managed to say before running away, toward the secret bathroom.

The Tide

On Tuesday after school, a day I had off from work, Susan drove me around Hopuonk on her mission to sell yearbook ads to different stores. It was supposed to take her mind off everything. Hopuonk looked smaller and crappier than it used to, the houses buckling in on themselves, the streets unplowed, the Christmas decorations sparse and outdated. With the Christmas lights up, it was easier to notice how many of the buildings were empty, and because all the lights were tacky, they showed the town's bad taste even more.

"How did everyone act at school after you kissed Scottie?" Susan asked, her eyes on the snowy road. She didn't quite smile, but the expression on her face was the closest I'd seen to happiness since her dad died. She hadn't come back to school yet, and she was avoiding Instant Messenger, so she didn't know the gossip.

I wasn't ready to tell her everything.

"Brad's really pissed-off," I said, stretching my legs out in front of me, feet on her dashboard.

I was smearing salt from the road and melted snow everywhere, but Susan didn't mind. None of us took care of our cars. Cars, to us, were just trash receptacles for holding our bodies and whatever waste we brought with us from one place to another. None of us went very far, and we were lazy. If we took the empty water bottles and Emmylou's cups out of the cars with us, we'd have to find a place to throw them away.

"But what did he *say*?" she pressed.

"Not a whole lot," I said.

"He must have said something," Susan said.

"He told me he loved me after your dad . . . you know," I said, "and I didn't answer him."

Susan reached over and shoved me, her expression both interested and fearful. I knew she was glad I didn't say it back, that I didn't love Brad, but knowing for sure that he loved me must have also hurt her.

"*How* could you not have told me this?" she said, turning up the heat in the car. Her cheeks flushed, bringing out the red in the cable-knit sweater that poked out from her black peacoat. We were both wearing the same outfit, all from Abercrombie, but my sweater was hunter green and my peacoat was gray.

I shoved her back.

"There's been a lot going on," I said.

"When I saw you and Brad go upstairs at the party," she said, "did you guys have sex? Did you finally do it?"

I couldn't bear to tell her about it, because I was embarrassed about how it felt but also because I knew she didn't really want to hear the details.

"You never tell me *anything*," she whined.

"That's not true," I lied.

Susan pulled into the parking lot of Gerald's Turkey Farm, where they sell Thanksgiving sandwiches year-round, little plastic containers of gravy, and also entire turkeys.

She got out of the car, then leaned in through the open door.

"We're not done talking about this," she said.

While I waited for her to come back, I bit my nails down to where you can't bite them anymore. Then I just sat there, waiting. The fact that her dad had just died, Susan said, would make the store owners more likely to buy ads.

Our yearbook was called *The Tide*. The name hadn't changed since long before Sandra went to Hopuonk High. When I thought of the tide, I thought of the awful smell when it was low—like rotten fish, like the inside of a dog's mouth. Tides have to do with the way the sun and moon line up, which decides how the water moves. We learned it all in primary school, along with everything about the Pilgrims. It honestly scared me—how everything was always moving, how space made decisions for us and for the starfish that washed up and got stuck between rocks in the tide pools, only to be picked up and prodded by children. But I guess it was a good name for the yearbook, really, because we were just like those starfish.

Hopuonk, at one point, had some kind of downtown where you could walk around, browse the shops, enjoy yourself. Scituate, the next town over, had a town center like that. Ours still had the buildings, but they were empty except for a Chinese takeout place; Ocean State Job Lot, which was where you went to get cheap stuff; and a surf shop that hadn't been repainted since the 1970s.

Instead of a real town center, everything in Hopuonk was organized by which beach you lived near, and which crab shack and ice cream parlor was next to that beach. Each one had its own packie to buy liquor and cigarettes and Hostess cupcakes and Slush Puppies.

If you looked at *The Tide*, you would see about eight million pictures of me. It made it seem like I'm everywhere, all the time, in the center of everything.

I was flipping through a paper sample of the yearbook that Susan brought with her to show the businesses.

There I was, at the junior semiformal, wearing a turquoise dress that showed my belly button. Sandra made me get it. And there I was, standing in the front row of Key Club—Hopuonk High's community service club. You know, the people who collect cans of food for poor people during Thanksgiving and Christmas, the people who tutor primary school kids who have trouble with reading and math, the people who tell each other how awesome they are. I only went to two meetings, but I was still in the photo.

And there I was again, in my Emmylou's apron, standing with Heather.

Heather also appeared a lot. In her cheerleading uniform. In her Abercrombie cutoffs. Standing next to her flashy new Volkswagen

Jetta. You mostly saw that she was blond and tall, that her boobs were big, and that she made duck lips constantly.

Then there was Susan, who was pictured less. The yearbook showed her on every court at dances, but always on the edge. There she was, between me and Heather, smiling without showing her teeth. There she was again, in the background of a picture of Brad in his lacrosse uniform, staring at his back.

The rest of the yearbook was predictable. There were a million photos of Brad, captain of everything. Then there was Scottie, the joker, in his Hawaiian shirt and oversized sunglasses. There was PJ onstage, wearing costume makeup, holding a bouquet of flowers padded with baby's breath.

Corvis was only pictured twice: once at the front of the National Honor Society photo, and one other time with Kristen.

The yearbook tried to capture everything, but of course, it couldn't. In the back, there were empty pages for us to write stupid messages to each other, which weren't any of the things we really wanted to say:

Dear Brad, I wish I could love you, but I'm defective. I hope one day you go to Asia and tell me what it's like, and let me know if it's real.

Dear PJ, I thought you were my friend. But you're not.

Dear Heather, why do you have to be such a bitch all the time? Why do I also feel like I want to show you what an orgasm feels like?

Dear Corvis, I wish I were you. Or not you, but like you. You're the only one who wouldn't switch places with me if you had the chance, and it makes me feel bad.

Dear Susan, I love you. Not like a friend.

Of course, I knew I would just write, Stay sweet, never change! and hate myself.

The Vampires

When Susan and I were six, we saw a family of vampires at Humming Rock Beach. We were collecting jellyfish and storing them in Sandra's cooler, and there they were—vampires. It was an entire family, all very pale, wearing black Victorian outfits with collars buttoned up to their chins.

"Oh my God, it's vampires," I said, dropping an armful of moon jellies.

"Vampires?" said Susan. She stopped in her tracks, salt water dripping down her skinny legs.

They walked past, not looking at anyone. In fact, it seemed like they were on a different beach at a different time.

"This is bad," I said. "They can turn us."

"How?" Susan asked. The littlest vampire was the scariest. He was basically translucent.

I didn't know how vampires turned people, so I didn't answer.

"Come on," I said. "Let's protect ourselves."

We started making crosses out of driftwood, wound together with seagrass. We placed them on our chests. When we got back to my house, we took the jar of chopped garlic out of the refrigerator and smeared it on ourselves.

Susan looked at me, tiny cubes of garlic all over her cheeks. "Do you think it's working?"

"I don't know," I said. "Pray."

That night in my bedroom, I kept thinking about vampires. I didn't want to be like them. I didn't want them to make me.

I understood later that they couldn't have been vampires. But we both remembered them that way.

Now, sitting in Susan's living room, I asked her about it again. We were both drinking Harpoon and wearing pajamas.

"They were definitely wearing Victorian clothes," she assured me.

But they were probably just a regular pale family, walking the beach in the summer, fully clothed. Maybe they were albinos. Maybe they were Amish tourists. The funny part of it, too, was that we assumed they were vampires instead of ghosts, which would have been a more logical explanation.

"Vampires can't be out in the daytime," I said.

"Oh my God, I know," said Susan. "What were they doing?"

"Brad broke up with me," I said abruptly. There was a look of relief in her eyes.

"For kissing Scottie?"

"I'm like a vampire," I said. "I suck everything good out of people. Everything warm."

Susan shoved me.

"What are you, a *poet*?" she said. "Elaborate."

I looked around the room—the worn leather sofa and love seat, the vaulted ceiling with exposed beams, the vase of dried flowers and cranberries on the mantel, the painting of Humming Rock Beach that Susan's mother made in high school hanging on the wall. I looked at everything—*really* looked—like I would never see it again.

I turned to Susan.

"It's complicated," I said, "and also not complicated at all."

Susan's face turned serious, ready. I don't know what she thought I was going to say—probably something regular: that I liked Scottie instead, that I was too afraid to give up my virginity.

It was time to tell her the truth. Susan Blackford was my best friend. Even if telling her would mean she thought I was disgusting, or if she didn't want to hang out with me anymore, being around her was becoming too much, especially since I no longer had Brad as a buffer. Even if Brad was now available, even if Susan might try to date him, I felt like I couldn't hide any longer.

"I think I'm a lesbian," I said, looking around Susan's living room as if there were an audience who might hear me. "I'm a lesbian."

Susan laughed. "You're not a lesbian."

Her face looked malarial in the low glow of the television. I settled my shoulders, thinking it wasn't fair to hurt Susan like this right after her dad died.

"I know what we can do," I said. "Let's make a blanket fort."

"But it's winter. We can't go outside."

I reached for the afghan at the end of the couch.

"That's okay," I said.

The Fort

The fort was a bad idea. I mean, Jesus Christ.

First of all, we got really drunk, so the fort was lopsided, and it made me dizzy to sit in it. Second of all, we didn't remember why this used to be so much fun.

"I don't remember how to *play*," Susan said. "Isn't that weird?"

"No, I know," I said. "When did we forget?"

Susan thought about it.

"Seventh grade," she said.

"Why was seventh grade different?"

"Because, like . . ." Susan reached up and touched the ceiling of the fort, thinking. "That's when we had health class, and they talked about abstinence and all, and we got scared. And Brad and Scottie didn't seem like our friends anymore. And we started going to the mall."

"I hate the mall," I said.

Heather gave a kid from Hanover a blow job in the arcade bathroom there. She still had his Red Sox hat.

"I hate my dad," Susan said. Then she laughed. "You're not supposed to hate dead people."

"You dad was . . ." I couldn't finish the sentence. Whatever he was, he wasn't that anymore.

"You tried to protect me," she continued. "You're, like . . . I don't know. You're so beautiful that it's hard not to get mad at you. I mean, Brad always liked you best. Everyone likes you best. I just want to *be* you. And I've always just thought that if I was close enough, I might learn how."

"*Why?*"

This was how I felt about Brad, in a way. If I could spend time around him, I might be able to learn what it was about him that Susan, that every girl, loved.

"You're Taylor Garland," said Susan. "Why did you pick me?"

I was starting to feel nervous. I looked at my stupid hands. The walls of the fort felt like they were closing in on us, like the air was getting thinner.

"I love you," I said.

Susan leaned over, sloppily, and put her hand on the inside of my thigh.

"I love you too, Taylor," she said.

"No," I said. "I mean, I *love* you."

We sat there for what seemed like seven billion hours, her hand just sitting there on my thigh, and then—I couldn't help myself— I put my hand on top of hers. I slid my fingers around hers, covering her hand with my skin. She was wearing a Claddagh ring, which dug into me. I moved her hand, very slowly, underneath my shirt, until her palm was covering one cup of my bra.

"Is this okay?" I asked her.

She looked at me, breathing deeply. She didn't answer, but she didn't protest either.

I knew this was probably wrong—I mean, since her dad just died, she wasn't thinking clearly. But the tension between us had been building for our entire lives, and if we didn't do something about it, I was sure that one of us would burst into flames.

She gently tightened her fingers around my breast. I thought this would hurt, like it did when Brad touched me, but it didn't.

With her other hand, Susan pushed down on my thigh, through the fabric of my pajamas.

Slowly, I leaned in close to her, my eyelashes brushing her cheek. The rest of the world dropped away, and I was left only with Susan, with the desire—maybe stronger than any other desire I'd ever had—to lick her face. Even in the moment, I knew this was the kind of thing animals wanted to do, to lick someone else, to taste them.

"Is this okay?" I whispered again.

"Yes," Susan breathed into my mouth, and I felt her muscles relaxing. "I like it."

She reached around me and unhooked my bra, then touched my skin. Her palm was sweaty.

"I like it too," I said.

I pressed my lips onto hers, too quickly. Our faces bumped together, and the knock of her jawbone hurt, but I kept going. I couldn't stop.

Susan's mouth didn't taste anything like I expected. It tasted like beer. But my whole body was in pain. This radiating kind. And then that pain disappeared. I felt her kissing my neck and my ear. Then her palm was on my belly.

I slid my hand under the elastic band of her white cotton underwear.

It felt boggy inside the fort we'd made, and the close air made me feel drugged.

Susan copied me, and though she was sweating, her hand was cold against my skin.

I put both of my hands on Susan's shoulders, pulled her on top of me.

"Is this okay?" I asked one last time.

"Don't talk anymore," said Susan. She yanked off her shirt, which caught on one of her earrings. Then she tugged at the bottom of mine and pulled it over my head.

"Okay," she breathed. "Go."

"Okay," I said.

Somehow, I knew exactly what to do in a way I never had with Brad—I knew to go slowly, to be gentle, to keep eye contact the whole time. Her skin was slippery and wet, and I could feel that mine was too.

When Brad touched me, I always felt hard and papery. Like a prune.

I looked at her eyes instead of asking her again if this was okay. Her eyes told me yes.

I moved my fingers up and down, slowly, then faster. Then I pressed.

Susan leaned back and closed her eyes. She made a noise I'd always wanted to hear her make, and I felt her pulse from the inside, which seemed like the closest you could get to another person.

I leaned over, my hair spilling onto her chest.

"You're perfect," I said to her.

I couldn't read her face. She looked at me differently than she ever had—like I had magical powers. She ran her forefinger over my lips.

"Let me do you," she whispered, sitting and pushing me onto my back. Part of her hair was stuck to her cheek, and the rest was sticking up like she'd been living in a jungle for the past month.

I hesitated.

Susan hovered over me, her cheeks flushed.

"I need you," she said. "Can't we pretend, just for one night?"

Maybe she wanted to pretend that her dad wasn't dead, or that she didn't hate him, and maybe she needed to put something big in front of it, to bury it.

"Yes," I said.

Slowly, she put her hand inside me. Somehow, she also knew what to do.

"Susan?"

She paused, her finger still, her other hand flat against my stomach.

"What is it?" she whispered, almost impatiently.

"I'm in love with you," I said. There it was. I needed her to hear it clearly.

She sighed, a little sadly. She kissed my forehead. She began moving her fingers again, and I felt like exploding.

She looked me straight in the eye and said, "I know."

My orgasm was like letting go of Rapunzel's hair.

———————

The next morning, Susan woke and immediately moved away from me. Her hair still stuck up on one side.

"Oh my God, I feel awful," she said. She looked me up and down, rubbed her eyes with her palms, and said, "What happened last night?"

She was a terrible liar.

"Seriously," she said, shrugging her shirt over her head. "I don't remember anything. I was so wasted."

I didn't say anything. I'd never even fallen asleep. The feeling of my hand inside her—and hers inside me—replayed over and over in my head; sometimes it felt really good, and other times it felt dirty or wrong.

She looked at me and shuddered.

"I need to take a shower," she said.

"Yeah," I said, pulling on my clothes as quickly as I could. It wasn't unusual for Susan to sleep naked, but it was something I never did, and we both refused to acknowledge it.

"Yeah," she said, "you should go." Her shirt was slipping off her shoulder, and she pulled it back up and crossed her arms over her chest, covering it.

I crawled out of the fort. This was the last fort—the last fort ever. I stood in front of it for a moment before I took off.

It was just a blanket, hanging crookedly over some chairs, falling in on itself. A mess.

The Space She Left Behind

When I got home from Susan's house, a full week after Susan's dad died, Sandra was lying on the couch with a floral cocktail napkin over her eyes, an empty bottle of vodka next to her on the floor, and the brown puke bucket. I hated the puke bucket—Sandra had first brought it out when I was a kid and had the stomach flu. It was about seven thousand years old, and we never used it for anything else.

"What's going on?" I asked. She could usually hold her liquor. "Red Red Wine" was playing softly, on repeat.

"He's gone," she said, her breath making the fabric of the napkin puff up.

You should go.

Susan's words had echoed in my head all the way home. I wanted more than anything to have a mother in that moment—a mother who wasn't lying on the couch with the puke bucket next to her, a mother like the kind you see on television, rushing around the kitchen, making breakfast, a mother who would listen to me.

If I could tell Sandra everything—what I'd done with Susan— maybe she would say I wasn't bad, that what I'd done was okay. She had sex. She didn't apologize for it. But she looked so pale that it seemed like one wrong word could send her over the edge.

If Johnny Moon were here, maybe he would comfort me. From what I read, there was no indication that he was Catholic, or an emotional basket case.

I sat down next to the couch and put my hand on Sandra's arm. Then I lifted the napkin off her face. Her eyes were swollen. The skin underneath was thin-looking, like tissue paper.

"Susan's dad?" I asked.

"Richard," she said, correcting me, "and he's never coming back." I saw that her eyes were red-rimmed, bloodshot. She'd been crying, and Sandra didn't cry.

"I know," I said.

"He was the only one who . . ." She started to say something, but then stopped herself. "Shit," she said instead.

"Wait," I said, taking my hand back. "Were you guys, like, doing it?"

Sandra took a deep breath and rubbed her temples.

"Oh my God," I said. "You were."

"Sometimes," she said, "I thought he was my one true love."

Those words sounded ridiculous coming out of Sandra's mouth.

"So it wasn't Mrs. Greenberg?" I said.

Sandra snorted.

"I can't believe I said that," she said. "*My one true love.*"

What Sandra revealed didn't surprise me. Mrs. Greenberg wasn't hot like Sandra. Still, I felt bad for her. She looked terrible. Was this how Corvis saw me?

"Brad dumped me," I said, changing the subject, maybe trying to relate, "but at least I have Stephanie Tanner. I've managed to keep her alive for eight years."

"Oh, honey," said Sandra, "Stephanie Tanner has died at least six times."

"Sandra!" I shoved her leg. "What?"

"I replaced her when you were at school."

"Did you just keep flushing her?"

Sandra wiped the hair out of her eyes, tucked it behind her ear.

"Actually, no," she said. "There's a Stephanie Tanner graveyard in the back, under the maple."

"Sandra," I said. "I can't believe you."

"Well."

I pictured her burying all the Stephanies, kneeling over the earth. She was being a mom, at least a kind of mom, whether or not she wanted to admit it.

I reached over and turned the tape player off.

"Susan's dad was an asshole," I said. "He hit her."

She touched my head, curled her manicured fingernails in my hair. Because she never touched me, I felt myself melting a little.

"He was an asshole," she said, "but he was gentle underneath."

The brown bucket was empty, which was proof that Sandra was

all right. She may have thought she wouldn't be able to handle the vodka, but she could.

"Sandra, I need to tell you something," I said. She had secrets too. Maybe she would listen to mine.

"Oh, Taylor," she said, massaging her temples. "What?"

I sat up straighter, looking her in the eye.

"I'm a lesbian," I said. "You were right."

It seemed best to do it this way—to tell her during a weak moment, so that she didn't have the energy to scream at me, or to cry.

She tilted her head, squinting at me.

"I thought so," she said absently. "You didn't react to Brad at all. The way he looked at you—you barely noticed."

"So you're not mad?"

As I said this, I realized that part of me had hoped she would be mad. It was so difficult to get a reaction out of Sandra.

"Just keep it to yourself," she said quickly.

I didn't say anything. I wanted her to banish me. I wanted her to slap me. I wanted her to call me a liar, to kick me out onto the street. Anything. Anything was better than nothing.

"I need to rest now," Sandra said, dismissing me.

I watched her back as she went upstairs, gripping the railing, white-knuckled.

I crawled onto the couch, into the space she left behind, the cushion still warm from her body heat.

The Haircut

I don't know. I guess I realized that I had never been to Provincetown before, and even though it was farther than Boston, it wasn't actually that far. The people there, maybe they could help me. I'd heard that people went there to be gay.

So, instead of going to school on Thursday, I just started driving. It only took three hours. I drove all the way down Cape Cod. Then the land thins off and becomes dunes on either side, and I thought I was lost. Even though there's only one way to go, I thought there couldn't possibly be a whole town there, but all of a sudden there was.

Susan came back to school, and she wouldn't even look at me. I tried to sit with her at lunch, and she got up and left. I sat there by myself for maybe two or three minutes, but then Heather sat with me. Then PJ. Then Scottie.

"We're wicked sorry we said that in the bathroom," PJ said, speaking for Heather too. "You know," PJ continued. "PMS."

Heather didn't apologize.

"Susan's acting weird," Heather said. We all watched Brad sit with her at another table, put his hand on her shoulder. "I know her dad just died, but still. She's sitting with *Brad*."

"So?" I looked at whatever disgusting casserole was on my tray. I thought of Susan's refrigerator, full of untouched casseroles just like this.

"So, you and Brad just broke up," said Heather. "She doesn't just get, like, a free pass to be a backstabbing slut."

Heather switched alliances quickly, and it was hard to predict which way she would go in a given situation, but today I realized she usually stuck close to me, even when she tried to hurt me. It occurred to me that PJ was the one who started the conversation in the bathroom.

"Yeah, she kind of does," I said. "She liked him before I did, after all."

I looked over at Susan again, sitting across the cafeteria with Brad. I panicked, for a moment, at the thought of her telling him everything. I remembered what happened to Corvis when we told everyone about her.

Then I wondered how much I cared. Part of me wanted someone to cut the thread I was hanging on to. Or maybe I just wanted to cut it myself.

"Whatever," Heather said. And then, "There's no way I'm eating this garbage. What *is* this? I can't even tell."

PJ put down her fork.

"I think Susan should be prom queen," I said, even though it wasn't even Christmas yet. People were already discussing prom like it was the main event of our lives. It was four months away, and everywhere you turned in the hallway, there was another girl describing who she secured as a date, or what her dress looked like. I figured that Susan would go with Brad, and that his tux would match her dress.

"Please," said Heather.

"What?" I said. "Don't you think she would make a good prom queen?"

Scottie shrugged.

"She's hot," he said to me, "but not as hot as you."

Heather rolled her eyes.

"Girl, I'm sorry," she said, "but you're going to be prom queen, even if you transfer schools. Even if you move to Australia."

———

Provincetown was empty. Commercial Street was lined with Christmas lights and wreaths, but it had rainbow flags flying everywhere too. Icicles dangling from the roofs. The rainbow made me uncomfortable. Was this where I belonged?

There were sex shops everywhere, above convenience stores, even. Vibrators. Strap-ons.

I wished Heather were there so we could make fun of everything and I could pretend sex was just a joke.

Every time I closed my eyes, Susan's hand was inside me, her hair brushing my chest, her breath on my face. The more distant that night became, the more I felt its realness. I woke in the middle of the night with crazy thoughts of going to Susan's house, crawling into bed with her like we used to, and kissing her.

I saw a hair salon down the street, next to an ice cream parlor, which was boarded up for the season. The salon was called Rock Paper Scissors.

I went inside and looked from chair to chair, but there were no other customers in the place.

A guy in high heels and makeup asked me if I needed help.

"Yes, actually," I said. "Can you just . . . Can you make me look gay?"

He smirked. I got the feeling that he'd been asked to do this before.

I felt like I was so far from Hopuonk. This guy would get murdered there. He had fake eyelashes and a wig.

"Sit down, honey," he said, gesturing to a swivel chair. "What do you mean, you want to look *gay*?"

"Just . . . make me ugly." Explaining it was too difficult.

He looked at my reflection in the mirror, and his expression reminded me of the one on Corvis's face on homecoming night in the secret bathroom.

"You don't really want to do this, do you?" he said. "Are you sure you're not just having a Riot Grrrl moment? I promise you'll regret it."

"Do it," I said. I closed my eyes. I couldn't watch. Also, his hands felt good on my scalp, and I went into a sort of trance.

The result was this: a half-buzzed head, the other half chin-length and wavy. It took about thirty minutes.

"This is what it's supposed to look like?" I asked when it was done. My face looked different. Staring at my reflection in the mirror, I felt like my skull was too visible, my nose too big, and my eyebrows too thick. I looked like I should be Kristen Duffy's friend.

The guy sighed and shook his head, placing a dainty hand on his narrow hip.

"You're more than just beautiful," he said to my reflection. "You're Brooke Shields beautiful. You're *Cindy Crawford* beautiful. Why'd you have to mess up that great thing you had going on?"

I stared at him in the mirror, at his makeup job. You could tell he was a cute guy, but his face was all covered with crap. I'd never seen a cross-dresser before, but why did he think girls had to wear fishnets?

"Well, why do *you*?" I asked. "Real girls don't wear fishnets, except on Halloween."

"I'm *not* a girl," he said, "and I'm not trying to look like one."

"Well, why are you wearing those clothes, then?"

"Because this is what I wear," he said. It seemed like he was enjoying this conversation a lot more than I was.

There still weren't any other customers, and I wondered what this man did all winter, what kinds of things he ate, where he hung out, whether or not he went fishing, or if he was an aspiring artist.

"How much for the haircut?" I asked.

"On the house," he said. And then, as I was putting on my coat, he said, "There's more than just one way."

"One way to what?" I asked.

He spun around, flinging a hand in the air, like I wasn't worth answering.

"One way to *what*?" I said again, but he didn't answer.

The buzzed side of my head was cold.

The Present

Sandra was still pretty beat-up about Susan's dad. We spent every Christmas alone, but this year, I felt a distance between us.

She was so upset about my haircut when I got home from Provincetown that she'd been ignoring me more than usual. I was hoping she'd yell at me, but she didn't. She was horrified and she told me it was ugly, but all she did afterward was force hats on me.

On Christmas morning, though, she didn't mention it. We ate powdered donuts from Bayside Donuts while we opened our presents, which was one of our traditions. We wore our pajamas and started drinking champagne at ten o'clock in the morning. By eleven, we were both pretty sloshed.

The tree was decorated mostly with ornaments I'd made as a little kid—Popsicle sticks covered in glitter, pinecone people, garlands of painted macaroni, and plastic cartoon characters hanging from strings, which came with McDonald's Happy Meals. We didn't have elegant glass bulbs like the trees at Heather's and Susan's houses.

I gave Sandra some makeup from Macy's, the expensive kind. Clinique. I only splurged on this once a year, and, as always, she pressured me to wear it, which was the second part of the present.

I was trying to compensate for something—my gayness, my haircut—I don't know. I realized that every year, when I spent part of my savings on expensive makeup, I'd always felt this way—like I was trying to compensate for who I was.

We didn't mention Susan's dad.

Sandra gave me a subscription to *Cosmo*—and a pair of clogs.

I didn't want them anymore, but I still felt like crying when I opened them. There was so much Sandra didn't know. What I really wanted for Christmas was for Susan to love me. Even more than that, I wanted a father.

I reached into the shoe box and pulled out one of the clogs. It was beautiful white leather, soft and expensive-feeling, with a wooden sole. I ran my fingertip along the stitching and thought about how I would probably break my ankle if I tried to wear them, just like Sandra had said.

"Am I too late?" Sandra asked.

The Hot Topic Kid

The day after Christmas, I begrudgingly went to the mall to buy a new pair of jeans while everything was on post-holiday sale. I went alone so it would be quicker, but I kept looking around for Susan. I didn't see her anywhere, and I hadn't heard from her either.

As I passed Hot Topic, I noticed Kristen Duffy, her arms empty, talking to that weird kid from our school who stood behind the register. I kind of lurked outside, then I full-on went into the store, ducking behind the rack of faux-leather jackets, and saw that Corvis wasn't with her.

"Your hair is, like, perfectly dyed," I heard Kristen say to the Hot Topic kid, leaning in a little too close. Today his hair was electric pink on one side and orange on the other. "Could you, um, maybe help me dye mine? I want to change it to green."

"Uh, sure," he said, his voice distant. "Or you could buy some Manic Panic, and your girlfriend could help you. It's not that hard."

I crouched down further so they wouldn't notice me.

"Cool," she said, "but, I mean, Corvis doesn't really know how to dye hair? Could you, like, come over this week and help me? I want it to be perfect." Her cheeks reddened, which confirmed that she was flirting. I noticed that her fingernails were painted black, and that she had rings on every finger. Her eyelids were heavily made-up with shimmering gray and pink shadow, her lips covered in a thick layer of purple lipstick. From her neck, a metal chain held a giant beetle frozen in amber.

It looked like it had taken her forever to get ready. She'd seemed confident with Corvis, but right now she looked like a terrified child, her posture liquidy, her shoulders slouching.

"Okay," he said, picking up on the flirting. "It's just, you guys seem pretty tight."

Kristen shifted her weight from one foot to the other, running her hand along the countertop. "Does Tuesday work for you? Anytime you're free would be cool," she said, ignoring his comment.

It was winter break, so we didn't go back to school until after New Year's.

"I have to check my work schedule," he said, which meant that he didn't want to do it. No one works all morning and all night. How did Kristen not pick up on his cues?

All of this seemed wrong, and it grossed me out that Kristen was so needy. I felt a pang for Corvis.

I forgot to buy jeans.

The Morning Shift

I think my dad is losing his mind," Heather said. "He's flying right now."

"On a plane?" I asked.

"No," she said, rolling her eyes. "On the wings of dawn."

We were making coffee at Emmylou's, and it was very early, before the customers were really awake. It was like a blizzard outside. Emmylou's should have been closed, but they never closed it down. Even in snowstorms, people needed their coffee.

"Oh, fuck you," I said. I held a handful of perfect little coffee beans. I liked to hold them. Once, when I was four, I got a coffee bean stuck up my nose and had to have it removed at the doctor's office. I was sad to see it go.

"He's taking *lessons*." Heather said the word *lessons* like she could smell it.

"Why?" I asked.

"Why." Heather smiled crookedly and spun around to look at me. "Well, why did *you* get that busted-up haircut?"

This was the first time anyone had mentioned it besides Sandra. No one from school who I'd seen over break had said anything at all. In fact, the only consequence of my stupid haircut was that a couple of days later, Bridget Murphy got the same one.

"Because," I said, "I kind of like it. I can feel the wind now. Half of it anyway."

"Girl, you're crazy."

"I know," I said.

"Susan still isn't talking to you," said Heather, hiking her black shorts. "I know she ignored us at lunch the other day, but whatever happened, I thought she'd be over it by now."

"She isn't."

"What happened?"

"I don't want to talk about it," I said.

"Come on," she said, placing her hand on my arm. "It's okay."

I sighed, and my breath caught on a jag in my throat.

"The other night," I began, then paused. I really wanted to get this out of me, this secret. "We, um, we did stuff together."

"What do you mean?"

"We kissed," I said, looking at my tennis shoes, which were worn in the toe and heel. "We kissed and then we did other stuff."

"*What?*"

"You can't tell anyone," I said. "It was like . . . she was sad about her dad, and I don't know. It just kind of happened."

Heather looked at me for a long time. She didn't exactly look surprised, and she didn't look angry either. I couldn't place the expression on her face. Sadness?

"Why Susan?" she finally asked. "Like, why her over someone else?"

"What do you mean?" I asked. "*Who* else?"

"Susan's just not as cool as you think she is," Heather said. She hiked up her uniform to show more of her thighs. "Also, why did you kiss Scottie?"

I shrugged.

"I don't know," I said, which was true. "I mean, he was there, and I needed something to change. Are you mad?"

"No," Heather said, smoothing down her top. She pursed her lips, checking her lipstick. "It's not like I have dibs on him or anything. Half the time I don't even want to have sex with him."

I wanted to ask her more about this. I wanted to know why she did it. I started to say something, but just then PJ burst in, her curly hair dusted with snowflakes. I was grateful not to have to answer Heather's question about why I kissed Scottie, which still hung in the air.

"Hey!" she said brightly, her voice about seven billion pitches higher than ours.

"Coffee?" I asked.

"Please, yes," said PJ, leaning onto the counter. "I was up so late after the play last night."

Her face still had stage makeup on it, smeared in places where she didn't wash it off all the way.

I made her favorite drink—Girl Scout Cookie—and just as I started handing it over, Heather snatched it away.

"Wait," said Heather. "In exchange for coffee, can you bring us breakfast sandwiches? I'm starving, and if I have to eat another pastry, I think I'll kill myself."

She held the steaming cup in the air.

"Oh," said PJ. "Sure!"

"Not from McDonald's," Heather said. "We want them from Bayside. With bacon."

"Okay!" PJ started to turn around. She was like Heather's little servant.

"Wait!" I called out to PJ's back.

She turned around.

"Coffee," I said, handing it over.

"Oh," said PJ. "Thanks!"

She disappeared. Soon, she would be back. She brought us anything we asked for.

I turned to Heather.

"Why are you such a bitch to her?" I asked.

"Because," Heather said, "everyone needs a friend who makes them feel superior."

"So mean," I said.

"Like you're any better," Heather said. "Isn't that why you string Susan along like a little puppy?"

"Susan strings *me* along," I said, and immediately regretted it.

"That's what I don't understand," said Heather. "You could choose from so many other people."

Like who? I thought. *Brad?*

"I don't want to talk about it," I said quickly. "Susan started it. She touched me first."

This wasn't necessarily a lie, but it also was.

She looked like she wanted to say something else, but I started making coffee again. We worked for several minutes in silence, and I thought about all the things you can't put into words.

"Do you think my dad is having an affair?" Heather asked finally. I was grateful to her for changing the subject.

I thought about it. Heather's parents actually seemed to love each other. I wasn't well versed on the topic of parent love, but her parents were the only ones I knew who still held each other's hands in public.

"No," I said. "He probably just needs to be in the sky. Or, like, feel something new. Anything. Sandra is starting to get older, and it's killing her. I wish she would take flying lessons."

"You think that's all it is?"

I thought of bridge jumping, of flinging myself off Fourth Cliff, and how almost dying or having the possibility of dying but *not* dying could make you feel real.

"Is that how your hair makes you feel?" she asked. "Or, like . . . is that how it felt kissing Scottie?" For a second, she looked like she might cry, but yeah, right. Not when she was sober. She reined it in.

I touched the buzzed side of my head. My skull, it turned out, was bumpy.

"Kind of, yeah," I said, "in a way."

"That makes sense," said Heather. She reached up and touched one of the rolls of lottery tickets, which seemed to hold all the possibility in the world.

Sometimes, while I drove to school, I would imagine that I won a million dollars and how I would spend the money—a new house for Sandra, a new wardrobe for Susan, a fleet of horses for me—and the money would be gone by the time I pulled into the high school parking lot. I was always disappointed that I'd spent it so quickly, even though it was only in my imagination.

"Heather?"

"What?"

"I can't do this anymore," I said.

"Do what?" She raised her eyebrows. I thought she was about to make fun of me, but instead she said, "Be here?"

"Yeah," I said. "I need to get out of Hopuonk."

Heather opened the cash register, getting ready to count the money before we started the day.

"Well," she said, looking directly into my eyes. She held a wad of bills in her hand, and for a second it looked like she was about to hand it to me. "I guess you'd better figure out how to go."

"What am I supposed to do?" I asked.

"Just go," Heather said.

Again, she looked like she might cry. Again, she stopped herself. She coughed—a fake cough.

"Don't worry," she said, looking down. "We forgive you."

The Last Letter

I wrote Johnny Moon one last letter.

It had been years since I wrote, so just in case, I inserted my senior photo in the envelope. It showed me sitting on the seawall at Humming Rock Beach, wearing a black dress that wasn't something anyone would wear to the beach on a regular day.

I explained the photo to him. I told him that maybe I looked nice in it—I was smiling—but that I wasn't nice. I was an asshole.

I told him how I kissed Scottie in front of Brad. I told him about how I didn't stop the other kids from egging Corvis's house. I told him that I had sex with Susan and probably broke myself.

I told him that Sandra was an asshole too. I told him that she had an affair with Susan's dad and then he died. I told him that I wondered if Sandra killed him.

Heart attacks have reasons. That's what they taught us in biology. You can ruin someone. You can ruin yourself.

I asked him to help me. I told him I needed him.

I told him I wanted to fly, like Heather's dad. I didn't belong in Hopuonk, and I didn't know how to get out.

I told him that he was robbed of the Oscar for *Mad Monk*. I told him that when I watched it in the theater, he made me cry.

I didn't expect a response.

Well, maybe part of me did.

Please, I wrote. *I know I'm yours.*

The Cold Coming In

After I finished writing the letter, I brewed two pots of coffee and drank one and a half of them. To calm myself down, I had a glass and a half of Sandra's rosé. I couldn't tell if that combination was making me crazy, or if I already was.

Then I got in my Volvo, planning to go to Heather's house to smoke some of her sister's weed. Instead, I took a sharp turn toward Juniper Hill Road, where Susan lived, my wheels screeching over the sand-covered pavement.

Susan's house looked unassuming when I pulled up to it—not the kind of house in which girls had sex in the living room.

I pulled into the driveway so fast that I almost ran straight into the garage. When I turned the engine off, I sighed, and my breath fogged up the window, like the sex scene in *Titanic*. I looked at my lap. I had Sandra's clothes on—a violet-colored crushed-velvet dress and a pair of black pumps—maybe in the hopes that they would transfer some of her fuck-everything attitude onto me.

I wanted to take my adrenaline and hand it to someone else—someone who needed it, like Brad.

Instead, I rushed to the living room window, and saw Susan and her mother sitting on the couch, watching television. They weren't touching, and each of them held a glass of blood-red wine. They stared at the television without blinking. Somehow, they hadn't heard me coming.

"Susan!" I shouted, banging a fist on the window.

She looked up. So did her mother.

"Susan, come here!"

She didn't. They both looked at me wide-eyed, blinking.

"Please!"

Her mother made a dismissive motion with her hand, asking me to leave. Susan leaned into her mother, like a child, burying her face in her mother's red terry-cloth robe. I could tell from the dramatic music from the television that they were watching Lifetime, and that the volume was turned up too loud, like they were trying to drown out the world.

"I need to talk to you." I kept banging my fists against the glass.

It just didn't feel right, us not talking. I knew something had cracked between us, something that couldn't be repaired, but without her, I wasn't sure who I even was.

Finally, her mother got up from the couch and came over to the window. Because the house was so old, they had single-paned windows like I did, which you could hear through.

"Taylor," Mrs. Blackford said sternly, looking at me through the glass. "Go home."

"Susan!" I called again. *"Susan!"*

Susan looked guilty, but she turned away from me.

"I love you!" I knew I sounded crazy, but it didn't matter. I was.

I'd read in *Cosmopolitan* that love turns you crazy.

"Go. *Home.*" Her mother's voice was both stern and tired.

I wouldn't.

Finally, Susan came over to the window too, bringing her wine with her.

"I'll handle this, Mom," she said, sliding the window open.

"I'll do *anything*," I said to Mrs. Blackford's back at the same time that she said, "Close the window. It's *freezing* in this house."

I wondered what she knew. Probably not much. Probably nothing.

"What." Susan's voice was tired, but stern. She looked at me through the open window, her cheeks flushed.

"Please talk to me," I said breathlessly. "I can't keep it in anymore. I can't hold in what we did in the fort that night."

"I don't remember anything," Susan said, taking a long sip of wine.

"Bullshit," I said. "You do. Otherwise, you wouldn't be avoiding me."

"Close the window!" her mother shouted from the kitchen.

I stuck an arm through the window, grazing the front of Susan's sweatshirt.

"Just, *please*." My voice was desperate. "Can I just come in?"

"You need to leave me alone," said Susan. Her face was stony, absent. I wished with every bone in my body that I didn't still think she was beautiful, but I did.

I felt anger blooming in my stomach, a fire burning down trees and houses, entire towns.

"Look," she said, her voice low. "I'm not going to talk about that night with you, or anyone else, and if you do, I'll never forgive you."

We stared at each other, a kind of challenge.

"You're just jealous," I finally said. "You've *always* been jealous, because you've always liked Brad and he always wanted me and not you."

I prayed that Susan's face would show me *something*, some indication that she loved me back, that it meant something to her, but all I could read was disgust.

"He loves me more than you, and he always will," I added. "No one will ever love you like I do."

She leaned in close, checking over her shoulder that her mother wasn't in the room.

"You actually are a bitch," Susan said. "Just like everyone says." She wiped her nose on her sweatshirt sleeve, blinking back tears.

I was already crying, which I hadn't realized. I'd never heard Susan call anyone a bitch before.

"So are you," I said. "You're just a different kind of bitch."

"I never want to talk to you again." Her voice was so sturdy, so sure. I felt like fainting.

"Close the *window!*" her mother yelled again.

"I'm sorry," I whispered as Susan slammed the window shut, almost banging my fingers against the frame, but I don't think she heard me. She disappeared into the house.

"I love you," I whispered into the air. My words turned into a cloud, then disappeared.

I stood outside their house staring into their living room until I couldn't feel my hands anymore. We'd sat on that couch together a million times, watching romantic comedies and sometimes the news, but only if it was juicy. I would have done anything to sit next to her again in the permanently indented spot where the springs gave in from too much use, to feel her body lean into mine, her head on my shoulder. I wanted to smell her.

I wanted to be anyone else in the world besides myself.

The Millennium

On New Year's Eve, we sat around Scottie's house, drinking and passing around a crooked joint.

Susan and Brad were together more and more frequently in public, and I knew that their closeness was at least in part to get back at me. In hurting them, I'd bonded them together. Brad was pissed-off at Scottie, too, so they showed themselves at the party but ignored the two of us. Still, Heather, PJ, Scottie, and the others clustered around me, like Brad and Susan were still in the solar system but no longer close to the sun.

"Two thousand years, man." Scottie held a tallboy in his lap, his other arm slung over Heather's shoulder.

"I know, right?" someone said.

Heather passed me the joint, and I took a hit. I was already high. Everything looked pixelated. The wallpaper in Scottie's living room, which had little flowers on it, was crawling with bugs. This stuff was definitely laced, but I didn't care.

I was afraid of the millennium. Just the word *millennium*, it sounded like the name of some galactic war.

"It must have sucked," said Scottie. "I mean, being alive two thousand years ago. I feel bad for Jesus."

Heather snorted.

"I don't know. Maybe it was kind of cool," I said. "Like, killing your own food, wearing fur. Caves are sweet." I didn't really know what I was talking about.

"I do like a good cave," said Scottie.

In the background, there was a game of beer pong. It was 11:17. I'd bought a little Y2K clock at the drugstore that counted down the minutes until the New Year. I was waiting to see what it did when midnight came. I was hoping for it to blow up, maybe shoot out some confetti and glitter or something. I placed it on the side table and glanced at it every few minutes.

Everyone talked about who they would kiss at midnight. I planned on kissing no one.

Susan was on the losing beer-pong team. Her dad never made it to the millennium, and she was still ignoring me. If I couldn't kiss her, I didn't want anyone. I had the clock.

"Your room looks like a cave," Heather said to Scottie. Scottie's eyes crinkled.

"Dude," he said. "I know it."

Did cave people sit around like this, talking about nothing? Probably not, I guessed. They were too busy worrying about what their next meal would be. I mean, the wheel wasn't even invented yet.

"Garland, your haircut is wack," Scottie said out of the blue.

Heather shrugged. "I think it looks sort of cool," she said, giving me the side-eye.

"Me too," PJ said. As always, she was the copycat.

"Why'd you do it?" Scottie pressed.

"I thought it would make me feel more alive," I said, "but I'm still bored."

When we were eleven, we spent New Year's Eve at Heather's house—Susan, Corvis, and me. At midnight, we walked down to the beach and jumped into the freezing-cold ocean in our underwear.

In the water, Susan's head popped up next to mine. We were screaming, and I could see little droplets of water on her eyelashes. We splashed to the shore, where our towels waited along with our winter clothes: long underwear, snow pants, Carhartt coats, puffy hats, Turtle Fur. We stumbled home, waiting to catch colds, our noses running.

That night, we thawed out in our sleeping bags on Heather's bedroom floor, talking in the dim glow of the Christmas lights that hung on the walls. We watched reruns of the ball dropping on the small television on her bureau. It was 1994.

In kindergarten, I asked our teacher when 1987 would come back. She laughed and said it wasn't coming back. Not ever. My stomach had dropped. I'd assumed it was some kind of circle, that the numbers turned around at some point and we returned to where we started.

"What does your prom dress look like?" PJ asked Heather now, and when I saw her gearing up to describe hers, I didn't think I could stand to hear about it one more time.

"Hey," I said to everyone, changing the subject. Scottie and Heather turned. "Hey!" I called louder, until everyone was looking at me.

The beer-pong game halted, the ball rolling across the floor.

"Let's go jump in the ocean," I said.

"You're crazy," Heather said.

"Let's go!" I shouted.

Scottie stood.

"I'm in!" he screamed, ripping off his shirt. If there was an excuse to rip off his shirt, Scottie took it.

"Me too!" said PJ.

Soon we were all running out the door, scrambling the one block to Humming Rock Beach, to make it before midnight.

We started stripping when we got to the beach, even though younger kids were there. I could feel the underclassmen staring, but we ignored them. This was our beach.

Maybe it was the drugs, or the fact that everything was ending. This was our last New Year's. Everyone had been talking about it for months, how all the computers would crash, how the world would end.

I left my underwear on. I hoped the computers did crash, and that we would have to start everything over again.

Heather started counting down the seconds until midnight, and everyone else joined in, then we ran into the ocean.

The water was shocking. I mean, *freezing*. I couldn't feel anything.

Heather popped up next to me and grabbed my shoulders.

"Jack!" she screamed, her voice wavering. "Hold on to me, Jack!"

We'd seen *Titanic* together two years before. Susan cried the whole time. I remember thinking, *How many times will they say "Jack" in this movie?*

Walking back onto the beach, I couldn't feel my feet.

"Never let go!" Heather shouted, pulling me down into the sand.

We were both shaking uncontrollably. I grabbed Heather, burying my face in her chest without even thinking about it. It was so cold that our nakedness was irrelevant.

Someone threw us a blanket. Heather caught it, and we fought each other for it, until we settled on hugging—the only way for both of us to fit.

"Stop trying to feel me up, Garland," Heather breathed.

"You're an idiot," I said.

Neither of our voices was back to normal yet. We both whispered breathlessly. This was the first time I'd ever hugged Heather.

It was 2000. From the beach, you couldn't tell what the computers were doing.

Back at Scottie's house, my countdown clock just turned into a regular clock. I would see no confetti. Nothing blew up. Scottie gave us pajamas to wear, and we sat around in the living room.

Susan got too drunk, probably on purpose, and I watched Brad lead her down the hall to the bathroom.

PJ had her guitar out. She was playing that Lyle Lovett song, "If

I Had a Boat." I felt kind of swimmy. Everyone sang along, in this desperate kind of way. We needed each other, but not for much longer.

That song, it's about going away. But the thing is, most of the kids at the party really did have boats—escape vessels—and all they did was take them along the brackish South River and dock them at Humming Rock Beach again.

I heard Brad and Susan's voices from inside the bathroom, but I couldn't make out what they were saying.

Heather sat next to me and looked at me with bloodshot eyes. She was drunk enough or high enough, or both, to wrap the blanket around me and scoot close. Our thighs touched. When she leaned in real close to my face, I could smell the alcohol on her breath.

"New Year's resolution," she said, turning toward the bathroom door along with me. "Let them go."

Something sharpened in my stomach. All along, I'd thought Brad losing his virginity to Heather meant they had some kind of special connection, when maybe it was just proximity that pushed us together. I wasn't sure exactly how Heather felt, or in what capacity she would be letting them go. I just knew I'd misjudged her.

PJ's voice was so beautiful. I kept imagining her on Broadway, which made me sad, because she'd already turned in her application to beauty school.

I tightened the blanket around us—Heather and me—and I almost started crying, but I didn't.

"I don't know if I can," I said.

It's funny how people think a holiday can erase everything—that you can make a resolution and it will matter.

This would be the first year since kindergarten that Susan wasn't my friend.

The smile left Heather's face, and she looked at me with rare seriousness. She touched my cheek, gently turning my head around to face her.

"You still have me," she said.

The Frisbee

On Valentine's Day, I was sitting on the seawall at Humming Rock when I saw Stinky Lewis, Brad's wiry little mutt, running across the beach with a tangle of seaweed hanging out of his mouth.

Then I saw why he was carrying it—a present for Brad, who stood there holding a Frisbee that Stinky Lewis seemed to have forgotten about.

My first instinct was to hide, but Stinky Lewis saw me and bolted, shifting his direction completely, coming straight for me.

His tiny head bumped my ankle, and I reached down to pet his chin. I loved his beard, his underbite. He had an air of confidence that no human possessed, and given how funny-looking he was, this confidence was endearing.

Brad jogged up, stopping six or seven feet from me, like I had a disease. Which I did, I guess. But it wasn't like he didn't have it too.

"No Frisbee?" I asked, not knowing what else to say.

Brad shrugged.

"He likes things that are alive."

We looked at each other awkwardly for what felt like seventeen million hours, while Stinky Lewis rubbed against my calf.

"How is she?" I finally asked.

Brad shrugged again.

"She's not great," he said, which answered none of my questions. I couldn't tell if he knew what Susan and I had done in the fort, or if he was referring only to her dead father. Susan could have lied to him about why we weren't speaking—why *she* wasn't speaking to *me*—but Brad's face didn't give anything away.

"I miss her," I said, still searching his face for some kind of clue.

He looked out at the choppy water, then let his arm fall to his side.

"Well," I said. "Take care of her."

Brad nodded. "I will."

"Okay."

"Okay."

A wave crashed against the shore and broke, pulling rocks back with it. I loved that sound. Actually, that's why the beach was called Humming Rock—because of that sound.

"Taylor?"

"Yeah?"

"She misses you too," he offered.

"Well," I said again. "I'm right here."

Brad considered this, then shot me a look of disappointment.

There is a power people get when they tell you they love you. It's a thing that can't be unsaid, a thing that forces you to consider them. You would think it would be the opposite, that the one on the receiving end had the power, but I was beginning to understand that it didn't necessarily work that way.

He leaned over, struggling with Stinky Lewis's leash.

"He wants to stay with you," he said to his shoes.

Stinky Lewis jumped up on my thigh, stretching his skinny legs against me. He made a noise that was halfway between a cry and a sneeze, then barked.

"I wanted to love you," I said to Brad.

"I know," he said.

Without completely giving it away, I think this was his way of indicating that he knew about me—of letting me off the hook. I didn't know if I deserved that.

"You're going to see her now?" I asked. Probably, he was bringing her chocolates.

This question hurt, but I had a morbid need to ask. I imagined it felt the same for Brad when we stood in the hallway the day we broke up, when he asked me if I loved him.

He didn't answer.

"Brad?" I owed him the truth.

"Yeah?"

"It's not that you're not perfect, because you are. It's just that I'm . . ."

His eyes widened. He looked both scared and frustrated, which reminded me of how I felt about him the night he jizzed on my leg.

"I know what you're going to say," he said, holding up his free hand, "but you don't have to say it."

I stood there staring at him, squeezing my fist into a ball to keep the tears in my eyes from spilling over.

"See you around," he said, pulling Stinky Lewis toward the parking lot.

As he walked away, I thought he looked so small, and in the wet, salty air, the smear of his red coat was like a painting.

The Horseshoe Crabs

I t *really* seemed like she wanted me to kiss her," I said to Corvis. I was driving us to Provincetown. Spring break, and we were both stuck in Hopuonk, just like everyone else except Heather, who was in the Bahamas.

Corvis had her feet propped on the dashboard. Her parents were away at a conference, so she wasn't worried about taking the day off.

"Well," she said, "of course she did."

"What makes you say that?" I asked.

"Curiosity," said Corvis. "It's really common."

"I think my heart is broken."

Corvis stretched her arm out of the open window and flicked her cigarette.

"I would say more like painfully chipped," she said.

It had been more than three months since the night in the fort, and Susan still wouldn't answer my calls. I called less often than before, but only out of embarrassment. At least three times a day, I dialed almost all of her number, then hung up.

That morning, I showed up at Corvis's house and demanded that we go on an adventure in Provincetown, now that it was getting warmer. Since we still weren't hanging out in public, I figured we'd better go somewhere else. Provincetown didn't go exactly how I imagined it would last time, and I thought Corvis would have something to add.

Corvis had been to a couple of other places. Disney World, for one, which she hated. Also, London and California. Her parents were the traveling kind of parents, not the kind whose family lived in Hopuonk their entire lives.

They were from Michigan. They chose Hopuonk because they thought it was *bucolic*, which means, like, pastoral and quaint—a place that makes you think of shepherds and things. Man, they had it wrong.

"I have dreams," I said. "Like, Susan and I will be in a rowboat or somewhere, and she just, like, jumps out. Or disappears, or turns into Leonardo DiCaprio."

Out of the corner of my eye, I saw Corvis's mouth set.

"Oh my God," I said. "Why am I telling you this?"

Part of why I wanted to go to Provincetown today had been to give myself some time away from the telephone, which was starting to seem like a monster. I spent too much time picking it up, putting it back down, and just sitting there, waiting.

"I guess because you're scared," Corvis said. "Which is okay. I am too."

"Of what?"

"What if I think college is going to be so great and it's not? What if I'm the dumbest one there? And then there's Kristen."

"What about Kristen?"

"She wants to come with me to New York," Corvis said. "She says she's in love with me."

I kept my eyes on the road, which was getting twisty. My Volvo protested, and I pressed the gas harder. Corvis sighed.

"She's not gay," she said.

I thought of Kristen's interaction with the Hot Topic kid at the mall. She looked at him the way Susan looked at Brad.

"But," I said, "you're always holding hands in public."

"She's not gay," said Corvis. "She's fat."

"So?"

"So she thinks she can't have a boyfriend because of it. Once she realizes she can, it will be different. She'll get married to a guy one day. She just doesn't know it yet."

"But do you love her?"

"I mean, yeah," said Corvis.

At least half of Corvis and Kristen's friends were in accelerated— headed to college, or at least community college.

"Which is why she can't go with me," said Corvis. "I can't just keep waiting for her to figure everything out."

Corvis kept speaking, looking out the window instead of at me.

"You and Kristen—you're opposites, but you have the same problem," she said. "You both let how you look dictate how you act, who you can love. And that haircut? Not the answer."

"So *how* do we stop loving them?"

"We can't," she said. "We live with it. I feel like shit, and I can't do anything but feel it."

"We did more than kiss," I admitted. "I'm not exactly sure, but I think we went all the way."

"Well," she said, "so have we."

"Does that make it better or worse?" I asked.

Corvis flung her cigarette out the window, a bit too forcefully. It almost blew back into the car with the wind.

"Fuck if I know," she said.

———

We wandered along the empty streets—even though rainbow flags lined it, Provincetown was still mostly closed-up. Maybe summer was a better time to be gay.

We ducked into a convenience store, where an ATM was lit by a giant rainbow. You couldn't tell if the person behind the register was a man or a woman, and they didn't greet us with more than a half smile before returning to their magazine.

A sign on a spiral staircase indicated that there were sex toys upstairs, and I tugged on Corvis's coat to follow me.

There were only a few aisles, but they were crammed full. My heart pounded, looking at the displays of objects that advertised vibration, or had strings or spikes attached to them for uses I couldn't even imagine. There was even a section for butt plugs.

"Do you need anything specific?" Corvis asked. She did not whisper.

"Shh."

I crouched in an aisle full of strap-ons of all colors.

"What are these for?" I whispered to Corvis, running my finger along a shiny purple one.

"What does it look like?"

"But, like"—I spoke very softly, hoping Corvis would catch on and copy me—"is it if you want a penis? Do *you* want a penis?"

"No, I don't *want* a penis," she said, still not whispering. "It's just a role. Here, I'm getting you one. You can read the instructions and try it at home."

"Try it on *who*?" I asked.

"You can use most of these things by yourself," Corvis said, as if I were an idiot.

"Do you and Kristen use these things?" I asked. "Never mind. I don't want to know."

Corvis picked up a solid-looking cream-colored one.

"This one's nice," she said. "It's German."

She carried it downstairs to the register and set it on the counter. It was sixty dollars, which seemed incredibly expensive, but Corvis didn't seem to think so.

"We're gay," I told the checkout person.

"We're not gay *together*," Corvis added.

"Right," I said. "Just next to each other. At the same time."

They gave us a strange look, and I saw Corvis's jaw clench. She shoved the bag into my chest, and we found ourselves back on the street.

"You're so awkward," she told me.

"Funny," I said. "That's what I was going to say about you."

Then I saw what I'd come here for—I just didn't know it yet. On the next corner, there was a tattoo parlor, and miraculously, it was open.

"Tattoos," I said. The strap-on touched my chest through the bag, and it made me feel powerful. "We're getting tattoos."

Excitement pulsed through my body, not just at the idea of getting a tattoo, but because Corvis and I had snuck away from Hopuonk in the first place and gone somewhere we weren't supposed to be, or at least somewhere my friends would never go.

I grabbed her arm and pulled her down Commercial Street with me.

I snuck out to Humming Rock Beach during the eye of Hurricane Bob when I was nine. I wanted to see what it was like, the calm part in the middle of everything. Everyone's power was out, and Sandra was holed up in her bedroom. All I had to do was walk out the back door.

After so much wind, the air was still and silent, but not the least bit peaceful. Stepping outside, I felt like a girl in a horror movie, singing in the shower, happy, just before the killer bursts in.

Down at the beach, the waves were bigger than I'd ever seen, like the ones in the paintings of shipwrecks everyone had in our houses. Usually, Humming Rock was more rocky than sandy, but this time, the shore was brown, moving. I remember it this way—every last inch covered with small bodies.

I squinted.

They were horseshoe crabs. Hundreds of horseshoe crabs were crawling back to the water after the huge waves had carried them all the way up the beach. They looked like walking helmets.

I'd seen them before, but usually only one or two at a time.

I was alone on the beach, except for a small figure in the distance. A girl in a red raincoat with a matching hat, kneeling in the sand.

She saw me and stood, cupped her hands over her mouth, and called, "Hey!"

It was Corvis.

Part of me was relieved—it was scary out on the beach alone, with the hurricane threatening to pick up again at any moment. The other part of me was irritated. I wanted to feel like an explorer, like sneaking out was mine alone.

Corvis jogged over to me, awkwardly jumping to avoid the horseshoe crabs, and met me at the seawall.

"Taylor," she said, out of breath. "What are you doing here?"

"I snuck out," I said. "You?"

"I saw them out my bedroom window," she said, gesturing at the bodies. "I'm going to save them."

I asked Corvis if they were made of armor. She didn't answer, but she did say that they had five pairs of book gills behind their appendages, which were meant for breathing underwater. She said that they could only breathe on land for a short amount of time, and even then only if their gills remained moist.

"Will they all die?" I asked her.

I was conflicted. These creatures were terrifying, like little aliens, but I didn't want to see them suffer. I didn't necessarily want to touch them either.

Most of them walked real slowly, tripping on rocks and getting trapped in the netting from dismantled lobster-trap carcasses. Their legs were so short that it didn't seem to matter how many of them they had.

"Not if we save them," she said. "Will you help me?"

I nodded, waiting for her to tell me how, but she didn't say anything. She just took off running, scooping up six horseshoe crabs at a time, piling them in her arms until they reached her chin. Her figure shrunk as she neared the edge of the water, her hat like a bright-red flame. I saw her open her arms and let them loose into the ocean, their legs waving goodbye to us.

"Save them!" she shouted at me, bounding down the beach and filling her arms with another load.

I froze.

"They can't breathe!" she called, but I just stood there without blinking as thunder started to roll again. The hurricane was moving back.

I squatted and picked one up by the tail, but then I saw its belly: a mouth centered dead between all the eggbeater legs, the bulbous claw, five pairs of eyes scattered throughout its body. An involuntary scream came out of me, and I opened my fist, flinging it away.

I gave a theatrical shudder, and Corvis looked back at me with drowning eyes, her raincoat blowing open at the throat.

It was a futile effort—one girl against a hurricane. No amount of determination would save every single one of these little dying aliens, but Corvis had to try.

Hurricane Bob would be one of the most damaging hurricanes ever to hit New England, and one of the costliest. Massachusetts was damaged more than anywhere else. Scottie's house was destroyed; same with lots of kids in my class. Both my house and Susan's, luckily, were on top of a hill. Most people evacuated Cape Cod, leaving the Sagamore Bridge completely blocked.

The storm traveled north to Maine, then New Brunswick, finally dissipating somewhere off the coast of Portugal.

It turns out that horseshoe crabs aren't even crabs. In fact, they're not even crustaceans—they're more closely related to spiders than lobsters. They can swim upside down, and, best of all, the females are larger than the males.

I didn't know any of this at the time; I only knew that the waves were angry, white-capped, and that horseshoe crabs were dying all around us. And, unlike Corvis, I could not touch them, because I was afraid.

———————

Now, at the tattoo parlor, we thumbed through binders of images — mostly red and black, or bright blue — of hearts, anchors, women who looked like pinup girls, dolphins, and symbols for *love* and *peace* in other languages.

"I've always wanted a tattoo," Corvis admitted.

The place was owned by a lesbian who was twice Sandra's age. I could tell she was a lesbian by her haircut, which was different than mine but, somehow, really gay.

"Are you looking for anything specific?" she asked. Her neck was covered in a primary-colored map, and she had an anatomical heart on her forearm.

I looked at her.

"Why did you put an *organ* on your arm?" I asked.

"It's a muscle," she said. "The heart is a muscle."

"It is?" I asked. This was a comforting thought.

"You didn't know that?" Corvis shot me a look.

"Shut up, Corvis," I said.

Realizing that you were supposed to be eighteen to get a tattoo, I told the woman, "I'm looking for something new for my twentieth birthday. Something to remember being a kid."

Beads of sweat gathered on Corvis's forehead.

I looked at Corvis and thought about how grateful I was that she was back in my life, and I thought of her that day during Hurricane Bob, her red hat bouncing in the still air.

"I know," I said, pushing the binder away from me. "A horseshoe crab!"

The needle felt amazing as it poked into me. I loved the pain of it. I looked at the woman's neck—like a map to find treasure—and watched the heart on her arm move. She didn't even ask for my ID.

After about an hour, I had a bloody horseshoe crab on my forearm. I ran my fingers over it, even though the woman had said not to touch it. Next, she covered it in ointment, then a plastic square, and told me not to get it wet for a week.

When Corvis's turn came, she shook her head.

"I can't do it," she said.

"Come on," I said. "You'll love it. It'll feel awesome to start college with a tattoo."

She backed away, looking faint.

———

Corvis and I lay side by side in the folded-down back seat of my Volvo, passing a bottle of Jim Beam back and forth. We were both too exhausted to drive home, and there was something pleasing about sleeping near the water with the windows open, listening to the waves dragging themselves up and down the sand.

"I feel like we're supposed to kiss," Corvis said into the darkness.

It's weird when you're right in the middle of a moment you know you will remember. Most things you forget. Meals, conversations, even moments that are really fun and amazing, but then there are these times—like when you're next to someone you love and won't see anymore, when your forearm is sore because it was poked with needles—that you know you will remember even as they happen.

"I know," I said.

"If it were a movie," she said.

"Actually," I said, "if you'd gotten a tattoo with me, and we had this, like, crazy experience together." Then there would have been no other way to extinguish the excitement.

"I guess so," she said.

"I wrote to my dad," I said.

"You found him?"

"Yes," I said. "I mean, maybe."

"Did he write back?" she asked.

"He never used to," I said, "but I have a feeling he will this time."

"I think he will too," said Corvis.

"I'm sorry you couldn't go through with the tattoo."

I meant it when I said it, but I was also glad, in a way. I touched the plastic square and felt a pleasant twinge of pain.

"So," I asked, in the foggy moment just before sleep, "do you feel like you belong here?"

"No," Corvis admitted. This time, she whispered.

"Me neither," I whispered back.

I knew I might never use the strap-on, but I also knew that I would open it every few days and hold it in my hands.

Remember? it would ask me.

It made me feel older, like I had more experience. I was a lesbian with a tattoo and a German sex toy.

"Corvis?" I whispered into the darkness just before I fell asleep.

"Yeah?"

"Is scissoring a thing?" I said. "Asking for a friend."

"No," she said, rolling over. "It's definitely not a thing."

"Wait," I said, on the drive back to Hopuonk. "So you, like, *love* Kristen Duffy?" I still couldn't wrap my head around it.

We were almost home, and the highway was ugly. It was late afternoon, which is the most depressing time of day.

"*You* love Susan Blackford?" Corvis said.

"So what?"

"She's worse than Heather Flynn," Corvis said.

She flung her Keds into the back seat and rested her feet on the dashboard. This pair of socks had tiny Popsicles on them.

"Susan has the longest eyelashes I've ever seen," I said.

"Kristen has beautiful cheekbones," said Corvis, "but that's not really what it's about, is it?"

"I guess not."

"It doesn't feel this way, but I'm pretty sure this part of our lives won't matter that much later," Corvis said. "It's just hard, you know, like, not knowing what else there is. Because there has to be something else."

It reminded me of Johnny Moon. People need movie stars to give them something to look up to. Like God. The people in Hopuonk felt the same way about me. They probably thought I didn't know, but I did.

"I'm not really a risk taker," said Corvis. "I guess I'm just a weenus."

"I guess you are," I said, shoving her arm. She laughed.

Sarah Lawrence wasn't as far away as it seemed. I mean, if you could just drive to Provincetown, you could drive anywhere else in the country. Or Canada, even.

After I dropped Corvis off, I came home to an empty house—Sandra was working. A letter addressed to me was propped against the coffee maker.

The Response

Dear Taylor,

To be honest with you, several of your letters reached me years ago, and there have been many occasions on which I sat down to respond, but did not, I admit, out of fear. This is not something I am proud of.

Some years ago, I had my assistant do some research on you. I've followed you loosely in the <u>Hopuonk Mariner</u> over the years. I was pleased to see that you were voted homecoming queen this fall, though I wasn't surprised.

In short, I think that perhaps you are right about our relation. I've always speculated about this, from the time I saw your fifth-grade school photograph. (It's in the nose.) You were wearing overalls with a paisley button-down underneath, and one of your front teeth was missing. I keep this photograph in a drawer in my office, and I take it out at least once a month.

This may be presumptuous of me, but I've enclosed a plane ticket to LA, leaving from Logan Airport, for the weekend after your graduation. I would like to invite you out here to visit, if you wish to meet. (I'll be filming in Vancouver until then.) I'd also like to introduce you to my agent. You have a great face, Taylor.

I myself did not know my father. He died when I was 18 months old—he was standing in the doorway of his friend's house when lightning struck the chimney, if you can believe that.

I appreciate your kind words about <u>Mad Monk</u>. Though, as you may know, that jerk Kevin Spacey beat me for the Oscar this year, the film did win Best Makeup. Kind of a consolation prize, if you ask me, but there will be more movies, more award ceremonies. Coming from someone who did not win, I urge you to take what is given to you. Your friend

Susan sounds lovely, but you seem to be the star. That is a good thing, Taylor. Your mother was the same way—the only person in the room, as far as I was concerned, whichever room she entered. I would ask you to give her my warm regards, but I think we'd better wait. The media is relentless.

I ask for your total discretion on all accounts mentioned in this letter, until a future, undetermined date.

It might be a good idea, also, if you didn't broadcast your feelings about Susan, or any other girls. I'm asking this of you for your own good—you wouldn't want the media to get wind of that.

Please burn this letter once you've read it. (I confess—I've always wanted to say that.)

All best,
J. Moon

The Orphans

When Sandra came home at two o'clock in the morning, I was sitting at the kitchen table with the letter in front of me.

She paused in the doorway. She looked so small and pretty, her face flushed and her hair wild, her forehead shiny with sweat.

"Mom?" I couldn't help but call her that. The word felt strange coming out of my mouth, like it didn't belong to me.

She didn't correct me this time.

"Why didn't you tell me?" I asked. I'd been sitting there for hours, and my feet were asleep.

She came inside slowly, closing the door silently behind her. She sat down across from me at the table without taking off her coat. Her hair was dusted with snowflakes.

"I didn't know for sure," she said. "When I saw that letter, though, I knew who it was from. Look at the postmark. Who else do we know in California?"

Her face was bright, awake. I realized she'd been going on adrenaline, and that maybe she was just as surprised as I was.

"How could you not know?"

She sighed.

"Honey, I'm not exactly proud of certain things I've done."

I raised my eyebrows.

"Certain *men* I've done," she said.

I nodded.

"Me either," I said.

We stared at each other. I slid the plane ticket toward her.

"What does this mean?" I asked. "What am I supposed to do?"

"It means your father wants to see you," she said.

"Can I go?" I asked. We both knew I didn't need her permission, but I wanted her to act like a mother.

"You decide," she said, "but I think you should."

"This is crazy," I said. I'd been staring at the kitchen wall all night, thinking about Johnny Moon—I'd never wanted to call Susan this much. I wanted to call her and tell her everything, but she wasn't my friend anymore.

I had a feeling that if I could get her on the phone, Susan would want to talk to me about this. That if she knew my dad was a movie star, she would take me back, at least as a friend.

Somehow, that was worse.

Then I thought of calling Corvis, but we'd just spent the past thirty-six hours together, and she didn't get a tattoo, and I was sure she was still upset about it.

I had Sandra to share it with. My mother.

"You'll have to tell me what California is like," said Sandra, smiling. "If everyone is actually made of plastic, if everyone wears high heels."

"Can you please tell me more about him?" I asked. "Anything at all?"

Sandra sighed.

"I wasn't sure exactly what he wanted from me. He was nice, but it was almost like he didn't live in the real world and he wanted to know what it was like. He came, he shook things up, it felt wonderful, and then he was gone," she said, "like a song you love that you know is eventually going to end."

I nodded.

"He bought us this house," she said. "He offered more, but I said no."

I had so many questions. If he bought us this house, he must have known about me. Why didn't he reach out sooner? Did he want to keep Sandra? Did she want to keep him? Did they ever talk to each other? Had he seen this house and picked it out for us, or did Sandra pick it out and send him the bill?

"So he's been here all along, in a way," I said.

"Yes," she said, "in a way."

Sandra's expression was almost wistful—and more alive than I'd seen since Mr. Blackford died. It was almost like she'd been wanting to share this with me for years, but didn't know how, or couldn't.

"I went to Provincetown," I said. "I got a tattoo."

Sandra's eyes widened.

"When?"

"Yesterday," I said. "It was amazing. Actually, it felt kind of good."

"You're just full of surprises, aren't you?" She sounded proud, which was the opposite of what I thought she'd be. She shrugged off her coat, letting it fall to the floor. "Don't you have to be eighteen to do something like that?"

"I'm almost eighteen," I said.

"Two and a half months," she said. "Then you won't have to steal my cigarettes anymore."

"Can you tell me everything you remember about him one more time?" I asked.

"I think this calls for some coffee," said Sandra.

She stood to make it, and I had this delicious feeling, like I was being cared for, but also like we were both adults, like we were friends. I watched the muscles in her arms jump as she lifted the pot and filled it with water, and I settled into my chair, the smell of coffee filling the kitchen.

———————

My eighteenth birthday was June 14, and by then, my life would be completely different, because I would have met my father. Graduation was at the end of May, which seemed both eternities away and also scarily close. Everyone's obsession with prom stemmed partially from the fact that they were still holding on while also trying to feel grown-up, as if floor-length tulle could age you, as if it could make you ready for what comes next.

I'd never imagined that Susan wouldn't be my friend when I turned eighteen—that she wouldn't be the one to make me a cake and throw me a party.

I kept thinking of my seventh birthday. Sandra asked me what theme I wanted my party to have, and I just said, "Old-fashioned."

She looked at me strangely, with her hand on her hip, probably wondering where the hell I came from.

"What do you mean?" she asked me. Then she asked if I wanted fifties diner food, doo-wop music, and poodle skirts.

"No," I said. "*Old* old-fashioned."

I explained: We would wear bonnets. We would use candles. We would drink tea with cubes of sugar—*the square kind of sugar*—in a china pot. We would eat salmon. We would jump rope. We would not use flashlights. We would say "alas."

This was the time when we had all just received American Girl dolls. I had Felicity, the colonial one, whose red hair was like Sandra's. This was where I got the idea for the party.

Sandra threw me the perfect old-fashioned birthday party. She actually made the salmon for us and laid it out on nice plates with asparagus and lemon wedges on top. She made little canvas bags and filled them with white street chalk, jump ropes, and paisley bonnets. One for me, one for Susan, one for Heather, one for Corvis. She built a fire and got one of her boyfriends to loan us a phonograph. None of us liked the salmon or the asparagus, but it was beautiful, and we enjoyed not liking it.

We sat at the dining room table, cloth napkins in our laps.

"Alas," I said. "My father died of cholera."

Susan put a sympathetic hand on my leg.

"My horse ran away," she said.

"I think I'm catching smallpox," said Corvis.

Heather leaned in, the bonnet slipping down her forehead, and she rearranged her face into a snotty expression.

"We are orphans," she said solemnly. "It's a good thing we have rich grandmothers to adopt us."

Even though it was eighty-eight degrees in my living room, we didn't use the air conditioner that night. Sandra laid out plain white sheets over the couch cushions, and even got us linen nightgowns to sleep in. We sweated and complained, and Sandra said, "You can't use what isn't invented yet, girls."

What Sandra gave me was a gift, a gesture in trying to understand me. Even though Sandra insisted I call her by her first name, she was my mother. I belonged to her.

The Prom

I carried the letter around with me—everywhere I went—in my wallet. Sometimes, in the secret bathroom, I took the plane ticket out and ran my fingers along the smooth edges of it—over the typed flight number, over my name.

Taylor Garland. Destination: Los Angeles.

Of course, Heather and PJ forced me to join the prom committee, and we had less than one month to make it "perfect." Susan wasn't on the committee, because Heather had taken my side.

I wasn't positive, but it seemed like Susan and Brad were together now. They sat together alone at lunch, and they didn't come to parties anymore. They floated through the halls like beautiful ghosts. Sometimes Brad held Susan's books.

Miss Donovan, the cheerleading coach, was our faculty advisor. We met in the health classroom on the first floor, and the prom, as always, would be held in the gym.

The health classroom was decorated with posters that made you want to puke. For example, one had two kittens on it, sharing a ball of yarn, and it said TEAMWORK! in pink script across the bottom.

Another poster had an unnecessarily graphic explanation of gonorrhea. I tried not to look at them.

At our committee meetings so far, I'd started suggesting the worst prom themes I could think of. The plane ticket made me feel reckless.

At one meeting that took place after last period one Tuesday, we pulled the desks into a circle. Everyone had an Emmylou's cup in front of them—some, like Heather, chose no whipped cream, because they were watching their calories. Others, like PJ, went for whipped cream *and* chocolate sauce.

Because PJ was a peripheral member of our group, it was her job to do the Emmylou's run. She sat with her spine straight, shoulders back, waiting for instruction. Miss Donovan, who smelled metallic, like cheap hair spray, looked like she needed a cigarette.

"Since we had 'An Evening in Paris' at homecoming, why not an evening somewhere more exotic this time?" I said.

Heather crossed her arms and looked at me.

"Like what?" she asked.

"Like . . . 'An Evening in Detroit'!" I said enthusiastically. Everyone was still obsessed with Eminem.

"You're insane," Heather replied. She had a notepad in front of her, because she was mostly in charge. She did not write down "An Evening in Detroit."

I suggested "Prom on the Moon."

"We can put trampolines everywhere," I said. "We can eat astronaut ice cream!"

Heather didn't write that down either. She glared at me, tapping her manicured nails on the table.

That was how, a week later, I got the committee to land on "Hollywood Dreamland." The "Dreamland" part wasn't my idea, but still, I liked the idea of Hollywood. We could make cardboard mountains, with the Hollywood sign on one of them. We could put posters that said the words *Director* and *Producer* over the restroom signs, which would confuse everyone, which meant I could go into the boys' room just to see it. We could have spotlights going back and forth, and a red carpet.

Our budget was crap, though. Miss Donovan showed up with a few cardboard boxes of dusty streamers, paint, Christmas lights, and felt, and told us to make the decorations from that. The stuff in these little boxes was supposed to decorate the entire gym.

PJ, unloading the contents of the boxes, frowned. She held a string of Christmas lights and looked at Miss Donovan.

"We were promised spotlights," she said. PJ, being the theater girl, wanted it to look realistic. She had been talking about the spotlights for days.

Duxbury, the rich town next to Hopuonk, had agreed to loan them to us from their theater department, but Miss Donovan now explained that since our lacrosse team beat theirs, all bets were off. We called them Deluxe-bury. They called us Hop-poor-onk.

"But . . . we were promised spotlights," PJ said again.

PJ was actually looking at me when she said this, like the whole thing was my responsibility, and therefore my fault. It didn't matter that I was not a lacrosse player, that I didn't even want to go to prom—the theme was my idea, and even if it hadn't been, I knew that everyone considered it my job to make things magical.

Not going to prom was not an option. Without the spotlights, everyone would have to try harder to imagine that they were in Hollywood, and while they were good at imagining, the gym was still the gym.

"Why are you looking at *me*?" I said to PJ.

"Can't you do something?" she said.

"I'm not a magician."

PJ slumped in her chair.

"This is so unfair," she said.

"Well, tough shit," Heather said. She leaned back and tossed her long blond braid over her shoulder like a whip, then folded her arms over her chest. "You'd better get used to it."

The red carpet was a long roll of paper, which was destroyed by high heels as my classmates walked through the door.

I wasn't wearing heels. I'd dressed as a director—my hair in a French twist, wearing a suit and oxfords from the thrift store out by the highway. I figured there was no way they'd queen me in boy clothes.

Susan, who still wouldn't look at me, who I missed so badly that every part of my body hurt, showed up with Brad. She looked perfect, in a sparkly red floor-length dress. Her hair was down, curled. Her eyelashes were so dark that you could see them from yards away.

My disease was threatening to come back. I had that tingling feeling you-know-where. It even hurt when I walked, where the seam of my underpants touched it. The pamphlet said it could come back with extreme stress.

I showed up to the prom alone, and got ready in the secret bathroom so Sandra wouldn't see me cross-dressing. I wore no makeup. I'd brought a handle of Smirnoff raspberry vodka with me, and I accidentally got drunk. I left the bottle in the secret bathroom, right there on the sink, still mostly full, hoping they'd find it and expel me.

The gym was dark, but the Christmas lights we hung didn't look like stars to me, even though I was drunk. They looked like Christmas lights.

The DIRECTOR sign was ripped off the boys' bathroom door less than an hour into the dance. The cardboard mountain we topped with the Hollywood sign looked like a mound of trash. The basketball hoops were too visible, and my classmates, all dressed in sparkly gowns and rented tuxedos, looked so out of place that it felt like I was in a strange nightmare.

Corvis, who was DJing, tried to play Counting Crows, Phish, Goo Goo Dolls, and Guster, but the drunker my classmates got, the more they wanted her to play rap. She reluctantly switched to Eminem, Dr. Dre, and the Notorious B.I.G., and as I weaved through the grinding bodies of my classmates—many of them making out right there on the dance floor—I wondered for a moment why a bunch of kids wanted to dry hump in public.

After a while, the music stopped abruptly, and I heard the murmur of over a hundred voices; everyone was anxious to see who would be voted king and queen. My classmates pulled themselves apart and turned to face the stage.

Miss Donovan tapped the mic. There was a horrible screech when she turned it on. She held it too close to her mouth, so her voice was painfully loud.

The crowns were illuminated on the folding table in the center of the stage, covered in the same paper we used for the red carpet.

Miss Donovan announced the court members, boys first, and Brad's name was called. He walked up and smiled tightly as Miss Donovan put the paper sash on him.

I watched Miss Donovan's mouth when she said that Scottie was voted prom king, and saw the lipstick on her teeth.

Scottie untangled himself from Heather and ran onstage, pumping his fist. The crowd cheered. Some people whistled. I wondered where they'd learned to whistle so loudly.

Then, Miss Donovan called Heather's name for court, then Susan's.

Last, Miss Donovan called my name for queen.

I got up onstage and stood there for a moment, looking at the rest of my grade, all in shiny evening wear. I was the only girl not in a dress.

Streamers drooped from the ceiling, reminding me of the inside of a car wash. The room smelled of alcohol and sweat, mixed with cheap perfume and hair spray. Even with the sparkly clothing, butterfly clips, dangling earrings, and tuxedos, this was clearly still a gym.

Honestly, school dances always smelled exactly like PE. The only difference was a false sense of excitement and the addition of vodka on everyone's breath.

I felt bad for my classmates. I mean, I just didn't understand why they needed to keep me on top so badly. There was no point anymore.

I grabbed the mic from Miss Donovan, even though you weren't supposed to make a speech.

"Congratulations, you fuckasses!" I shouted. I felt dizzy and weak, and the crowd in front of me wavered under the lights. I couldn't see individual faces, just a bunch of made-up eyes and glitter.

Everyone stared at me in silence. I'd had way too much raspberry vodka. My lips were moving, but I couldn't control them.

"You have your first gay prom queen," I said.

There was some chatter, people looking at each other, waiting for me to keep going. Miss Donovan reached for the mic, but I held on to it.

"I'm leaving this fucking town," I said. "I'm going to California. My dad is a movie star. Johnny Moon? Maybe you've heard of him? He's my dad, and he's taking me away. I'm never coming back."

Johnny Moon had only invited me for a visit, but I'd be so lovable, I thought, that he'd let me move in with him.

There were gasps all around. More chatter. I couldn't tell if my classmates thought I was delusional or if they believed me, or both.

I spotted Mike O'Malley in the crowd—the kid I'd left on the dance floor back in middle school.

"By the way," I said into the mic, "Mike O'Malley doesn't smell like cheese puffs, so you can all stop calling him Cheese Puff Boy. I just didn't want to dance with him because I'm a dyke. He's actually really nice, and he smells fine."

Miss Donovan tried for the mic again, but I gripped it with all the strength I had. Everyone was still staring at me, waiting.

"Susan!" I shouted. I turned to her—she stood on the side of the stage, next to Heather.

"*Taylor*," Miss Donovan hissed at me.

"Susan, I love you!"

Susan looked horrified. She shook her head, reached for Brad's hand. My stomach went sour. Susan didn't need to go to California. She had what she wanted right here in Hopuonk.

"I love you, Susan!" I cried desperately anyway.

Someone finally dragged me off the stage.

Corvis, at the DJ station, locked eyes with me. I thought I saw a hint of pride in her expression. To dissipate the tension, she blasted "Girls" by the Beastie Boys.

The music blared, and I ran away as fast as I could. I tripped on the staircase leading out of the gym, but I kept going until I was in the parking lot.

I sat down, which hurt.

I was going to need another round of herpes-suppression pills. I was going to have to go back to the doctor who had given me birth control—the same doctor who gave me the prescription the first time—and she was going to inspect my body all over again.

I could still hear the music inside the building. It sounded too hopeful, which made me even more depressed.

The Spotlight

I was still sitting outside in the parking lot when Heather came out and sat next to me.

"Go ahead," I said, pulling a cigarette from my pocket. One great thing about suits were pockets. "Make fun of me."

Heather had on a white dress that looked like it was meant more for a wedding than a prom.

"Nah," she said. "I'm sick of that." She took a flask out of her bra, unscrewed the cap, and handed it to me.

I took a sip, and whatever it was burned bad on the way down.

"So you're actually saying your dad is Johnny Moon."

"Yes," I said. "My dad is Johnny Moon."

"You're shitting me," she said, shoving my leg with hers.

I sighed. "Nope."

I pulled the plane ticket out of my pocket—it was the only thing in there besides a pack of Sandra's cigarettes. I handed it over.

"See?" I said. "He sent that to me."

Heather leaned back against Bridget Murphy's rusty Bronco—the closest car—holding the plane ticket up to her face. She handed it back.

"Wow," she said. "You probably have about seven million half-siblings running around."

I shot her a look. I hadn't thought of that, but I knew she could be right.

"Think about it," she said. "I'm just being honest. And there's something else I need to be honest about."

I waited for a long time for her to say something, and when she didn't, I lit my cigarette.

"Spit it out, Flynn," I said.

"I would totally make out with you," she said.

"You're drunk," I said.

"No . . . I mean, yeah. I am. But I've always thought you were, like . . . I don't know. I don't want to like you, because you're prettier than me . . . but there's something that's just kind of magical about you, like you aren't real."

"I'm not magical," I said.

"Yes," she said. "You are. And I've tried to stay away from you, but I can't. And I get it. I know I'm just another person out of about seven billion other people who say this to you all the time."

"Say what—that they would make out with me?"

"No, that they like you. Because I do. I think I like you. I like you."

"What?"

This was the last thing I ever expected Heather to say to me.

She looked down, her shoulders slumping over. She wouldn't

look at me. Instead, she started chewing her nails, which, normally, she was morally opposed to. She slipped her feet out of her heels and, with her toes, pinched a few blades of grass that were growing out of the asphalt.

Images of Heather flashed through my head: Her in the air, getting basket-tossed at halftime, her spirit fingers stained with nicotine. Heather dressed as a dead beauty queen on Halloween in fifth grade, wearing wax-candy lips. Heather when she didn't have time to put on makeup before work, when you could still see her freckles.

I reached over and touched the tulle of her dress, pressing down until I could feel her leg.

Heather pushed me away and waved her hand dismissively.

"It's fine," she said. "I know you're in love with Susan and not with me. I don't know what crushes even are anyway, but everyone says they're not real."

"A crush is a person who you always want around," I said, "and when you see them, your stomach does a flip, and their eyelashes kind of make you want to cry."

"What I don't understand is," Heather said, "why *Susan*?"

I didn't say anything. I just drank more from the flask, and then I passed it to Heather.

She took a long sip.

"I used to think . . ." I stopped. "I guess I just . . . don't really know anymore."

"She's not good enough for you, Taylor," Heather said.

When I thought about it, Susan had never been interested in me as an actual person. She wasn't even someone I could talk to. Suddenly, nothing made sense.

"Let's drink it all," I said. "I want to be sick."

"So do I."

We did drink it all, and we waited to be sick but weren't.

Finally, Heather felt a little sick.

"Where's your car?" she asked me. "I need to lie down. It's all spinny."

I pointed, and Heather walked over, weak-legged as a colt, opened the door, and sprawled herself across the back seat. I climbed in after her. We barely fit, and our faces were only an inch apart.

"Prove it," I said, probably a little too loudly.

"Prove what?"

"That you would make out with me."

Heather sighed and pressed her face into the door handle.

"I can't," she finally said.

"Why not?"

"It'll either make me fall in love with you and then you'll leave, or it'll make me realize I'm just experimenting and then you'll get hurt. And you'll still leave."

"Heather," I said. "Didn't you see what I did in there? I can't stay here now."

"Well," she said. "Your plan worked out."

"I guess so."

"I'm not, like, *gay*," she said, trying to clarify. "This is just a weird stage or something. Don't we all go through stages like this?"

I thought of Heather's entire demeanor, the way she wanted us to think she breathed sex and power. She had a perfectly curated character she presented to everyone, and she executed it well.

We all had secrets. We did our best to keep our own, and to keep each other's.

"Come with me to California. I'm pretty sure I can convince Johnny Moon to let me stay with him, and you can live with us," I said. "You don't really want to stay here. What do you actually want to be?"

Heather sighed.

"Fuck if I know," she said. A few moments passed, and then she said, "I want to be a makeup artist. Like, for famous people and models, okay?"

I felt brave, so I took Heather's hand and squeezed it, then kept it. She didn't take it away.

"You can be," I said.

"Yeah, right," Heather said. This close, I could see a small freckle on her ear, and the scar from a cartilage piercing that was now closed-up.

The streetlight shone directly on us, like a spotlight.

"You're going to get a shit ton of money," she said. "Your life will be so fancy."

"I'll buy you a pony," I said. I was still holding her hand.

"Taylor?" Heather turned to face me. Our noses almost touched.

"Yeah?"

"Not that this isn't something you don't already know," she said, "or that it even matters, but Susan isn't smart. In fact, she's kind of an idiot. You need to forget about her."

Heather's breath smelled like alcohol and peppermint Altoids. She kept a tin of them with her at all times.

"I have herpes," I said.

"Well," Heather said, smirking. "Now I'm definitely not making out with you."

"It's on my you-know-what, not my lips."

"Not convincing, Garland."

It felt good, telling someone about the disease I had. Since it was Heather, that meant everyone else in Hopuonk would know soon too. Surely, once the whole town found out, that information would mean that my reign was over—if I hadn't already ended it at prom.

"I *am* going to California," I said. "All this time, I didn't really believe it. The weirdest part is that even though he sent me a letter, I've never even spoken to him."

"I always knew you would go somewhere else," she said.

"How?"

"This place is too small, and everyone expects too much. They can't help it. It's how they're wired."

"If I can't be here, which I can't, then why am I scared to go?"

"How could you not be?"

"Why do I feel so guilty?"

"You have to go," she said. Miraculously, she put her arm around me. "You'd make a terrible dental hygienist."

"Heather?" I turned and pressed my nose into her neck. It smelled like Clinique Happy and sweat.

"What?"

"I really love you," I said. I realized this only as I was saying it, but I meant it in a different way than I did when I'd said it to Susan. Heather was someone I respected. She was strong.

"You're a dildo," she said.

I felt like we were floating, like my Volvo was a submarine and the parking lot was the ocean. Heather fell asleep, and I listened to the sound of her small, shallow breaths. Her body relaxed into me. Her hand, still in mine, twitched. I didn't move.

Through the window, the moon looked like a coffee stain in the sky.

The Shrinking

A few days after prom, I got a phone call from Veronica Michaels, Johnny Moon's assistant. I sat at the kitchen table squinting at the empty notebook in front of me, which I was trying to fill with an essay about *Gulliver's Travels*.

"It's for you," Sandra said, handing me the phone. I hadn't heard it ring—I'd been daydreaming about changing sizes, changing personas.

I looked at the paper in front of me and saw doodles of starfish and octopi surrounded by hearts, which I hadn't been conscious of drawing.

I took the phone from Sandra.

As Veronica Michaels explained to me that Johnny Moon wanted to visit Hopuonk the following week for a photo shoot of us in *Vanity Fair*, I looked around the kitchen and noticed how shitty my house was. The windows let in cold air, the countertops were water-damaged and lumpy, and the refrigerator gasped like it was exhausted from running a marathon. I didn't want him to see this house, even if he did buy it.

"He'll be flying from Vancouver on his two days off, which are

Tuesday and Wednesday," Veronica explained, "and they'd like to shoot you both on Humming Rock Beach, and several other locations around town, for a reunion piece on the two of you. They'll also want to interview you beforehand. It'll be *great* publicity."

"But," I said, playing with my pencil, "we haven't even reunited yet."

"It'll be wonderful!" said Veronica, ignoring my comment. "He's *so* looking forward to meeting you. He doesn't want to wait until June."

My heart started pounding a little, and I thought of my secret plan to convince him to let me move in with him. I needed more time to figure out how to make myself more charming than I was, more like a daughter someone as famous as Johnny Moon would want to keep.

I looked down at the plane ticket, which sat in front of me on the table. I still had to wait until after graduation to use it.

When I was little, maybe three or four, Sandra used to take me to Logan Airport for lunch, to watch the planes take off while we ate.

We sat by the window, and while I took bites of a burger that was too big for my mouth, she would say, "That one could be going to London, or Florida, or California."

I realized now that it was a weird thing to do, to take your kid to the airport for lunch, then drive home.

At first, I didn't understand that people went on the airplanes—

I thought they were just big metal toys. One day, though, I saw people waiting in a line outside, to board a particularly small plane—one that was too small to board from the terminal. I realized that the planes were full of people, that they were not toys but vessels that brought people from one place to another. This was terrifying to me.

I watched the tiny plane take off, my hamburger uneaten on the paper plate in front of me. Just like the others, the plane got tinier and tinier, until it was invisible.

Sandra noticed the look on my face—pure fear—the expression I've seen on children's faces, or even my friends' faces, when they finally get around to understanding something new.

"What's wrong, honey?"

I looked at her. Then I pointed to a line of people waiting to board another plane.

"Those people—is this when they shrink?" I asked Sandra.

That fear I felt back then, when I watched those people shrinking into the sky, was how I felt right now as I listened to Veronica rattle off a bunch of logistics: Where Johnny Moon would be staying—a hotel in Boston, because Hopuonk only had one motel and it was dingy, though she didn't say that. The name of his agent. The kinds of questions the *Vanity Fair* reporter would be asking me. She didn't ask me if I had a biology final on that Wednesday, which I did, not that I cared.

"But we haven't even met," I said. I wanted to ask if I could talk to him. I wanted to know when he would start loving me. *If* he would start loving me.

"This will be great for *both* of your careers," Veronica continued. "You'll be on the cover, and of course, there will be a significant center spread."

I looked at my empty notebook again. I didn't have a career. I was seventeen. I couldn't even bring myself to write a coherent essay on *Gulliver's Travels*, and I was still failing math.

It was strange, the amount of planning that went into his life. I wasn't sure I wanted this man—my father, the movie star—to come to Hopuonk. I wanted to go to him instead. I wanted to start fresh.

All week at school, no one had talked about anything except Johnny Moon. Bridget Murphy, who usually didn't feel entitled enough to talk to me, came up to me in the hallway and bombarded me with questions about him, none of which I could answer. A few freshmen asked for my autograph. Susan still hadn't spoken to me, but I saw her staring during study hall. It felt like it had always felt— everyone's eyes on me—only *more*.

No one mentioned my gayness. Johnny Moon was bigger than my gayness.

"They'll send wardrobe people out the day before," Veronica said. "You can keep the clothes afterward!"

"Wow," I said. "Cool."

After we hung up, I felt deflated, which made no sense, because this was literally every girl's dream, wasn't it?

I also felt like a fraud. I felt both like I deserved a father and also like I didn't deserve for a big magazine to interview me, because I was bad at school and I wasn't even nice, like Susan and Brad.

I stood to get a beer from the fridge, and went outside to sit on the stoop in the freezing cold. I thought of Heather's face on New Year's Eve, just after she popped up out of the ocean.

I realized that when Sandra handed me the phone, I'd wished it had been Heather calling.

The Crown

The day after Veronica Michaels called me, I was lying in bed, watching Stephanie Tanner dart around the plastic castle in her fish tank. Sandra knocked on the door lightly before appearing.

"Susan's downstairs," she said.

I woke up with a cold, and I'd been sleeping the whole morning. I dreamed about Heather. We were playing this nationally televised game where we had to get across the ocean in a tiny green rowboat and all we had to eat were Froot Loops.

Heather, though she'd been distantly friendly lately, was mostly avoiding me. I guess I knew too much now. She'd even switched some of her shifts at Emmylou's so we didn't work together.

My bedroom used to make me feel trapped, but now it was comforting. The ceiling slanted down, creating the same familiar shadows every afternoon. Susan and I painted the walls sky blue when we were twelve, intending to sponge-paint clouds to make it look like the sky, but we never got around to doing the clouds. The blue came out too bright, so I covered the walls with posters and collages that Susan and Heather made me in middle school — magazine cutouts of models, clothing we wanted, the words *Friends* and *Beauty* and *Gossip* shellacked over photos of us at the beach or the mall. Dust motes swirled around in the dim light of my knockoff Tiffany lamp, which sat dutifully on my vanity, next to my prom-queen crown.

I rubbed the sleep from my eyes and told Sandra to send Susan up.

There she was in my doorway, looking smaller than she used to. Her eyes were red, and she was wearing a baggy sweatshirt with NANTUCKET across the boobs. Her hands were shaking. Mascara was caked under her eyes, like maybe she'd been crying.

"Hey," I said.

"Taylor," she said, "I'm pregnant."

Stephanie Tanner rushed behind her little plastic castle.

"What?"

"Yep," she said, running her forefinger down my door frame.

"Shut the door," I said. I made space for her on my bed, like I'd been doing for practically my whole life. "I have a cold, though, so sit at your own risk."

When we were kids and Susan got the chicken pox, I watched her from the bus stop, standing in the picture window in her bedroom, wearing a white nightgown. She looked like a Victorian ghost. Immediately after school, I rushed over to get the chicken pox from her. All week, while we stayed home from school, we pretended to be Victorian orphans with the measles. "I'm cold," I said over and over, and she answered, "My mother is coming one day." We even made Cream of Wheat and pretended it was orphan porridge, and that it was the only food we'd had in weeks.

That was back at the beginning of my obsession with being anyone other than myself—a pirate, an orphan with the possibility of different parents, of living in another time. Now that I actually had a famous father, it felt uncomfortable—not at all as I'd imagined it as a child.

Susan sat down, blew air from her cheeks. She didn't necessarily look unhappy, but she definitely looked scared. She smelled like Salems and strawberry lip gloss, not like herself.

"It's Brad's," she said. "Obviously." There was no hint of anger in her voice, no resentment. She was probably a little bit proud.

A few months ago, this would have sent me down a spiral. Now I felt surprisingly solid. Even though it was strange, and maybe even a little bit shitty, I had a way out now.

"How pregnant?" This was a stupid question, but it was the only thing I could think of to say.

"I mean, there's a baby in there," she said. And then, "God. I missed this room."

She looked around, squinting at one of the collages she made— the one she gave me at my fourteenth birthday party at the pizza place in the mall. We got in a food fight with my cake, and the manager made us mop everything up, then kicked us out.

"I thought you'd never come here again," I said.

She leaned back, letting her arm touch mine. I'd been waiting for this to happen for months, but now I was too sick or too different to feel anything.

"I haven't told Brad yet," she said.

We both stared at the popcorn ceiling. It looked like the top of a frosted cake.

"When are you going to tell him? You have to tell him, Susan."

She settled into my pillows, which were covered in moist tissues. Then she extracted a Salem from the front pocket of her sweatshirt and lit it with a crooked match. When the flame went out, a delicate strand of smoke twisted toward the ceiling.

"I know this is bad," she said, holding up the cigarette but meaning all of it. Everything.

I sneezed.

"I'm sorry," I said, "but maybe . . ." I didn't finish. I wouldn't keep the baby, but this was Susan.

"My mother says it's a blessing," Susan said.

Well, she would, I thought. I already felt like the ground had dropped away, and I was afraid for Susan. I don't know if I was surprised, though.

"That was some prom speech," Susan said, exhaling smoke through her nose like a dragon.

"God, what a mess," I said. I pulled my legs to my chest. "I hoped you'd get queen," I said. "You deserved it."

Even as I said this, I realized that it wasn't true—it should have been Heather. It always should have been Heather.

Susan shrugged.

"They can't have a pregnant prom queen," she said.

"Well, they have a gay one."

We sat there for a while, both of us considering apologizing, I guess—me, for kissing her, for touching her, for always having what she wanted, and her for touching me back and then ignoring me. But for me, apologizing would have meant being sorry for existing, and I just wasn't.

"I'm sorry I was such a bitch," she finally said. "It just freaked me out when we, *you* know." She couldn't bring herself to put words to what we'd done. And then she said, "I really love him."

"I know you do."

"He'd rather have you. I know that," she said, "and I shouldn't have blamed you for it."

"No," I said. "You shouldn't have."

"God," she said.

"God," I said.

"Can I sleep over?" she asked.

I honestly didn't want her to. My chest felt heavy, my nose plugged-up, and I wanted the freedom to be gross by myself. Heather popped into my mind again, the smell of Clinique Happy, the way it felt lying next to her.

"Yeah," I said to Susan. "Of course you can."

"Is everything going to be okay?" she asked me.

"I don't know," I said. I took the cigarette out of her hands and threw it out the open window. This time, I told her the truth. "I've never known the answer to that, Susan."

Then I got back in bed beside her, pulling the covers over us like I'd done so many times before.

"I bet the baby will have your eyelashes."

Susan gestured toward my vanity, at the prom crown. The homecoming crown was long gone, probably buried under Susan's bed.

"It's nice," she said. This crown was a step up—it was plastic instead of cardboard. In the middle were little blue and red rhinestones.

"I guess I'm a fuckup," I said. I wanted to go back to the night of prom, when Heather had let me hold her hand in my car. I should have kissed her, but then again, look where that got me with Susan.

"Well," she said. "At least you're still pretty."

"I wish . . ."

I wanted to tell Susan how distant Johnny Moon felt, how none of it was going the way I'd imagined it would. Then I realized that I never had discussed those kinds of things with Susan—around her, they were only thoughts.

"I don't even know what I wish," I said.

"I can't believe your dad is a movie star," she said. "When is he coming to Hopuonk?" I'd been waiting for this, and I wondered if it was the real reason she came over. I didn't want to talk about it.

"Next week," I said. "He can only come on the two days he isn't shooting."

"What is he *like*?" Susan asked.

I paused, still looking at the ceiling. "He's like a stranger," I said finally. "He's like a unicorn." As I heard Sandra's words come out of my mouth, I wondered how much I was a part of her, how much of me came from being her daughter.

"You're so lucky," she said.

For the first time, I realized that Susan didn't respond to things I actually said. She had conversations with herself—she only wanted comfort, praise, and attention. And whatever it was that I had. I felt sorry for her.

"Susan," I said, turning to face her. "Tell me how it happened. It'll make you feel better. That's why you came here, isn't it?"

"Okay," she said. "You're right."

She told me the whole story. It was prom night. What a cliché.

They'd been sitting on Brad's bed. Susan was crying about her dad, her mascara running down her cheeks. A painting gone wrong. She was hugging one of his pillows. They started talking about me and my speech. She told him that I kissed her. She left out the rest.

"We started kissing, and he was sweet," Susan said. When Susan started unhooking her bra, Brad said, "Wait."

This is when he got up and started pulling candles out of his desk, the candles that had probably been meant for me. He lined the windowsills with them. He covered every surface with them. Then he walked around the room with a match, carefully touching the flame to every wick.

Next, there was the music. The music that was meant for me too. A Dave Matthews Band CD.

She thought having sex with Brad would be better than when she lost her virginity to Scottie at one of his parties two years ago, she explained, and better than when she had sex with lots of the other boys in our grade too.

This time, there were candles.

"Brad was so wrapped up with the candles, with making me feel better, that he forgot the condom. After we were done, he told me he loved me," Susan said, propping herself on my pillow. "I know he was lying, but I said it back anyway. I tried to convince myself he really did love me."

I blew my nose.

"What makes you think he didn't mean it?" I asked her.

She ignored my question, saying instead, "I'm not even sure if the actual experience of being with him lives up to what I imagined. I think I made it too big in my head, too special. Everything he did was right, but it somehow felt weird."

I reached over and took her hand in mine, squeezing it. There was a lot I wished I could say—that I felt the exact same way about Johnny Moon, that I was afraid meeting him would ruin the image of him in my mind, that I understood how she felt—but we just weren't the kind of friends who shared those feelings anymore.

Maybe we never were.

The Father

As it turned out, Brad did tell Susan about the herpes. He was taking suppressants. He didn't kiss her unless it was safe. So far, nothing seemed to be happening to Susan, except that she was pregnant.

He told me this on the phone. When Sandra called me down into the kitchen to take the phone, she seemed surprised that he was calling.

I looked at her and shrugged, then shooed her out of the room.

"Meet me at Damen's Point," he said when I answered. "It's important. I have something to give you."

I didn't want anything from him. He'd already given me herpes.

"I'm right in the middle of doing my homework," I lied, and I'm sure he knew I was lying, because I didn't do my homework.

"Just meet me there, Taylor," he said desperately. "Please. Ten minutes."

When he showed up, Stinky Lewis was with him. The dog kept spinning in circles, full of nervous energy. He rolled over for us, even though we didn't have any treats. After that, he presented each of his paws.

"I need you to take him," Brad said, instead of hello.

Susan's pregnancy was public knowledge now, so there was no need to discuss it. Everyone at school was talking about it, and Susan acted like it was this amazing thing, like it was exactly what she wanted.

When I saw her, she smiled curtly, but she never slept over again. I was there when it was still an accident, and she needed to erase me.

Johnny Moon was coming soon, to do the shoot, and the atmosphere in Hopuonk was exactly as I imagined it had been the first time he came—the time when I was made.

"What do you mean, *take* him?" I asked Brad.

"I'm going to be a dad," Brad said. "I won't have the time." His plaid shirt was buttoned all the way up, and he wouldn't really look at me.

We sat in silence for a few moments, listening to the waves break and watching Stinky Lewis.

"I've only ever had a fish," I said. "I can't take care of a dog."

"Taylor, just take him with you. I won't be able to stand seeing him around."

The news of my move was part of the gossip too. As usual, I didn't have to tell anyone what was going on in my life. They already knew. Worst of all, Johnny Moon didn't know I planned on moving to California. Panic welled inside me.

Brad's jaw was set. It seemed like this had been Susan's idea. Even if it wasn't, Brad could probably feel that it was what she wanted.

Stinky Lewis sat at our feet, his ears forward, eager. He wagged his tail twice, then once just halfway, like he was losing confidence.

"Brad, I'm sorry," I said, "for everything."

When we stood on the prom stage together—him with his court sash and me with the crown—he wasn't expecting my explosion. He stood there politely, then backed away. I didn't blame him. At the time, I was so focused on Susan that I didn't pay much attention to anyone else, but I realize now that he must have felt exposed somehow too.

Brad picked up a gray stone from the ground and threw it at the brackish river. Even though we were all the way on the dock, it reached the water. It always amazed me how easily boys could throw things, and how far.

"You hurt me," he said.

"I know."

"I'm sorry I told you that everyone hates you."

"It's true."

He didn't argue.

"You'll be a good dad," I said. "I know you will be."

"I think it's what I'm supposed to do," he said. He looked out at the water instead of at me when he said, "Right after Susan told me she was pregnant, Heather gave me a blow job."

That stung, for several reasons. I thought of Susan stretched out in my bed, telling me the story of sleeping with Brad and getting pregnant, going through tissue after tissue. She seemed so small, and she thought of Heather as a friend. Knowing about Heather and Brad would have undone her. And Heather said she liked me, but she wouldn't kiss me. I understood, and I respected her more for not doing it, but Brad got to kiss all the pretty girls.

He picked up another stone and ran it through his fingers. He didn't throw this one.

"I'm a bad person, aren't I?" he said.

I shook my head.

"Lots of people would run," I said. "I mean, from the whole baby thing. One blow job isn't the end of the world. Just don't tell Susan."

"I thought about running," he admitted. "But I don't want to. I want to do this." He sounded like he was trying very hard to convince himself.

Stinky Lewis barked and clawed at my sneakers.

"He likes you," Brad said. "That's my cue."

There were tears in his eyes that he clearly didn't want me to see, and I didn't want to see them either. I looked instead at the river, a hungry, grabbing thing.

When he got up to leave—he left his blanket—Stinky Lewis whined. I held him back on his leash. Stinky Lewis raised his ears again, wagged his tail, and then sat down.

Brad turned around, his hand on the door of his Datsun.

"Taylor," he said, "good luck in California."

"Thanks."

How would I convince Johnny Moon to love me? I wondered if he liked dogs. I wondered if he liked goldfish. I wondered if he liked pirates.

Stinky Lewis looked at me, confused, then looked at Brad's car. He barked as the car pulled away.

I think Stinky Lewis was nervous, because he started rolling over for me, right there on the dirt. It was like he had to prove that he was worth keeping.

"It's okay," I said to him, curling my fingers into his wiry fur. "Stop rolling over. You don't have to roll over. I want you."

The Hopuonk Beachcombers

A few days later, after my cold had passed, I found myself walking out of school, not to the parking lot, but to the field, where one of the last cheerleading practices of the season was being held.

There was Heather, the team's best flyer, her horsey knee bent ninety degrees on top of a pyramid. When she cheered, her face took on a brightness that I never saw at any other time.

I watched for a while. The Hopuonk Beachcombers actually had a fantastic cheerleading squad. They went to nationals, which were held at Disney World every year, and though a couple of teams from Kentucky always beat them, they usually placed pretty high.

I watched Heather as the two bases basket-tossed her high into the air, and I wondered if cheerleading, for her, was like her father's flying lessons were to him. Then I watched her on the ground, effortlessly performing a full twist after two perfect back handsprings.

No one ever watched cheerleading practice, and I knew that Heather's dream of winning at nationals and bringing home a ring would never be realized. But I also knew that this wasn't her only shot at being really good at something.

I wanted to tell Heather everything I felt. I wanted to tell her that

Johnny Moon did not seem like he'd be the father I was hoping for, that all of it felt weird. I also wanted to tell her that she'd been in my dreams, that I probably liked her—that I liked her but didn't know if she liked me back.

She noticed me and jogged over.

"What are you doing here?" she asked breathlessly. Her bun was loose—slipping to the left side of her head. Blond tendrils, curled from sun and sweat, hung around her face.

"Can't we just be friends again?" I said. "I don't like anyone else."

"What do you mean?" she said coolly. "We *are* friends."

But we both knew that something had changed on prom night. The power had shifted, and neither of us knew in which direction.

She looked me up and down. I was wearing overalls—men's overalls, left over from one of Sandra's boyfriends. The overalls matched Stinky Lewis. When we walked together, I looked like a hobo and he looked like a hobo's best friend.

"That's not true, that you don't like anyone else," said Heather. "It seems like you're pretty into Corvis McClellan these days."

Had she seen us together?

"I heard you took a trip with her over spring break," Heather said, shifting her weight from one leg to the other. "When did you start hanging out again? Do you *like* her or something?"

I sensed jealousy, maybe even a little hurt, in her combative tone. It fueled me a little.

"Yeah," I said, shrugging. "Maybe I do. So what?" Part of me wanted her to think I *like* liked Corvis, to make her jealous, and part of me wanted to punch myself in the face for being such a pussy, for not just kissing Heather right there on the practice field.

"I thought you didn't like anyone else," she said, shifting her weight.

I stared back.

We stood for a moment, daring each other to say something else, but neither of us could bear to be the weak one.

"I have to get back," said Heather. She turned and walked toward the squad, silently practicing cheers as she went, clapping, punching a fist toward the sky, practicing, practicing, practicing, though the competition was already over.

The Floral Dress

The next morning at Emmylou's, I told Heather about Stinky Lewis and she told me about Brad. She couldn't avoid me at work *all* the time, and I got the feeling that she wanted to tell me about it anyway. To put me in my place. To show me she wasn't in love with me.

"Brad gave me his dog," I said when she walked in the door. "Out of nowhere. Have you seen him lately?"

Heather raised her eyebrows and handed me a cup of coffee.

We stared at each other for a moment. I took a sip of coffee, then another.

"I gave him a blow job," she finally said, pouring a giant paper bag of coffee beans into one of the plastic containers behind the counter, labeled REESE'S PIECES. She filled each plastic container by flavor, which we did so our supply looked full to the customers.

I acted like I didn't already know. I didn't want her to think Brad was going around bragging about it, because he wasn't—he told me because he felt guilty. Plus, I was mad at her for doing it, and I wanted to hear her side of the story.

"What happened?" I asked.

She handed me the next giant paper bag, labeled GIRL SCOUT COOKIE, like she couldn't tell a story and work at the same time. She shrugged.

"He showed up at my house like a sad little puppy," she said. "He was wearing a flannel that was too big for him, and he looked like he'd been crying."

She hoisted herself onto the counter, dangling her long legs. She wore inappropriate shoes for working—three-inch black pumps.

I filled the coffee containers while she talked.

"He said he didn't want to go home, that something bad had happened," she continued.

"Susan told me about that," I said, just so she would know that I knew my gossip. "I don't think that's going to work out so well."

Heather rolled her eyes.

"Yeah, well, he was pretty upset," she said. "And I guess I wasn't feeling awesome either."

"Why?" I asked, setting down a bag of coffee beans.

"I don't know," she said. "I mean, when I woke up in the back seat of your car the morning after prom, I felt kind of shitty. That night, I went to Scottie's house and made out with him behind the boathouse in his backyard. And then behind the willow tree. And then behind his car. I thought about that time I gave that kid a blow job at the mall, and how we'd been in the bathroom, behind an unlocked door. I just felt like . . . so much of my life is spent behind things. I think it must be some kind of metaphor."

She barely ever said this much to me, so I stayed silent and tried to make myself smaller.

"So when Brad showed up at my house, I asked him if he wanted to talk about it, which made me sound like a guidance counselor. And I know I'm not the kind of person people look for when they need actual help. It's like, I only have this one thing to give them."

Heather and I both felt bad for guidance counselors. They were doomed to fail, because they were adults, and the only people teenagers wanted to talk to about their lives were other teenagers. The guidance counselor at Hopuonk High, Mr. Doyle, was fairly innocuous, and he truly seemed to care about the students, but we could feel his desire to sleep with us, and even though he'd never done anything about it, it canceled out any of his already tenuous credibility.

"My parents were fighting upstairs," she continued. "And I didn't want to think about it, so I told Brad to come inside for a beer, even though he was already drunk."

I was afraid to interrupt her. She took a deep breath and scanned the parking lot for cars. There were none.

"Does Brad come to you a lot when he's upset?" I asked. I had a suspicion that maybe he did—that maybe she'd given him blow jobs while he was *my* boyfriend. If I asked her about it outright, in this moment, she would probably admit it. But I didn't want to know.

"Not really," Heather said, shrugging. "He lost his virginity to me, so he has an *attachment*, I guess. But it's not conscious."

"So, what happened next?" I asked, leaning against the wall, giving her as much space as I could.

"When I came back from the kitchen with the beer, Brad was pacing up and down the hallway. That's when he said it, when he told me Susan was pregnant. I guess she'd just told him about it that day. Meanwhile my mom was yelling at my dad to leave her alone, and when I asked Brad if I could do anything for him, he basically said it would be awesome if I could blow him. He said it just like that. Like, 'If you could give me a blow job, that would be really cool.'"

Heather stared at her new shoes and smacked the heels together. She wouldn't make eye contact with me, and she looked like she might cry.

It was hard for me to picture Brad actually saying that out loud, but I knew people treated Heather differently than they treated me.

"It was gross," she admitted. "I mean, I didn't know where to go, so I shoved him into a coat closet and he sat down on this random stool. My knees hurt on the hardwood floor, and my mother's furs were in the way. After a minute, he came all over the front of my Laura Ashley dress. I loved that dress."

She twisted her index finger around in the fabric of her hot-pink Emmylou's T-shirt.

I knew which dress she meant. It looked great on her. Usually, Heather wore bland clothing from Abercrombie or American Eagle—clothing that was tight. The point was to show off how sexy she looked in the same outfit everyone else wore. The Laura Ashley dress was old and faded, just a bit tight at the waist but loose and flowing everywhere else, falling just below the knee. It had belonged to one of her older sisters.

"Why did you do it?" I asked her.

Heather laughed, but it was a sad laugh. She looked at the ground. We hadn't swept yet, and tumbleweeds of pine needles and dust were gathered on the tile.

"Because I could," she finally said.

That was exactly what I'd said to Susan about the time I kissed Scottie at The Mooring, and it was a lie.

"Really?" I pressed. "Because that doesn't seem true."

"Fine," she said. "I just wanted to make him feel better. I didn't know how else to do it."

When she finished telling the story, we both realized we were still mad at each other. She stood and walked across the room, reaching for the heavy wooden broom we kept in the closet. We worked in silence for a while, the broken radio cracking with every base beat. The song "As I Lay Me Down" by Sophie B. Hawkins came on— the most annoying song in the world.

"I hate this song," said Heather, reading my mind. "It's literally *always* on."

"In the background, it sounds like she's saying 'I love tacos,'" I said.

"It totally does," she said.

Heather was sweeping, and her hips were slowly moving along with the music as she swung the broom back and forth.

I grabbed the remote control to the boom box, using it as a microphone. Heather and I started singing, and we turned to face each other just in time for the part that's like, "On a summer evening, I'll run to meet you, barefoot, barely breathing," and just like that we were dancing together, and everything else floated away. When it got to the taco part, we both shouted it at the top of our lungs.

By the time the radio voice interrupted, we were both out of breath, laughing. We collapsed on the floor.

But then Heather said, "My parents *are* getting divorced. They told me last night."

"Heather . . ."

Her shoulders heaved, and she let out a big ugly sob. I loved that sob. I wanted to kiss that sob.

"Okay," I said carefully. "It's okay."

Then she let me hold her. She gathered my hair in her fists and leaned her weight into my chest. Her body shook so hard that I thought she might break open. I wondered what happens to your organs when you don't let anyone hug you for years. I held on tight.

"I'm sorry," she said, clutching my arm. "I'm sorry I did that to Brad, and to Susan, and to you."

I didn't feel angry anymore. The sleeve of my Emmylou's shirt got drenched in tears and snot.

The Dollhouse

When I went to Susan's house for what would be the last time, she was sitting in front of her dollhouse. I brought a present for her baby, a blanket Sandra bought at the Ocean State Job Lot. The tiny chandelier in the dollhouse dining room lit up Susan's face, and because she was looking down, her eyelashes made little shadows on her cheeks.

Next to her on the floor, I saw a tuna fish sandwich, half-eaten.

"Susan."

My voice startled her. She dropped a tiny roasted chicken made of polymer clay.

"Sorry," I said. "Hi."

She looked at me, picked up a porcelain man, and opened her hand, her palm like a starfish, letting him drop to the floor. Something in him cracked on impact.

"He's going away," she said ominously.

"Which one is he?" I asked.

"He's the grandfather," she said, her tone serious and calm. Her hair was shiny, her skin smooth, but she looked exhausted. "Now I call him death by suicide."

Slowly, I moved toward Susan and sat next to her, setting the blanket on the bed. I thought of Susan's dad hitting her with his belt.

Susan flipped off the lights in the dollhouse, and it went dark.

"That story is over," she said. "There's a new one now."

I picked up the man doll from the floor and cracked his head off. Susan sighed and took a bite of the tuna fish sandwich.

"We're getting married," she said, chewing. "Brad asked me to marry him."

"Congratulations," I said, and it came out kind of like a question.

"My baby is the size of a blueberry," she said, "and this baby's dad isn't going to be like mine. Things are going to be better for it."

"Yeah," I said, not knowing what else to say. "She'll be okay."

I thought I remembered hearing that you're not supposed to eat tuna fish while you're pregnant, but I let it go.

The New Name

I t was past midnight, and I was in bed with Stinky Lewis, sweating. He wanted to cuddle, but it was hot. He seemed nervous since Brad left him with me, and I wanted him to feel better, so I cuddled with him anyway.

Suddenly, I had an overwhelming urge to find my Schwinn. I sat up in bed and switched on the light, which was jarring. My bedroom was messy, and the bottles of Clinique perfume and makeup on my vanity were embarrassing. The posters and collages on my wall were embarrassing too. I felt both too old for everything I owned, and like a child.

I wore an oversized T-shirt that belonged to one of Sandra's boyfriends, with the KISS 108 FM logo across the front in puff letters. I grabbed a pair of dirty corduroys from a pile on the floor and yanked them on, then pulled the long half of my hair back into a messy bun.

The bike had to be somewhere in the garage, which is where we kept everything we didn't use but couldn't get rid of—like an ugly set of crystal that had belonged to Sandra's parents before they died, and the boxes of Christmas decorations. We were not people who used crystal. We were people who drank out of Solo cups.

When I finally found the Schwinn under a pile of wooden lobster traps, something in me loosened. There it was, faded by sun from hot pink to a pale-salmon color, the basket splintered, the banana seat covered in a thin layer of mold.

I grabbed the handlebars, ran my fingers through the fraying plastic ribbons, and pulled the bike out into the driveway.

I looked ridiculous riding my Schwinn, even though it was too tall for me when I was seven and I'm still short.

No one was watching, though. Almost all the lights were out in the houses, and we didn't have streetlights on this side of town.

The bike was so rusty that it wailed as I pedaled. I'd had this feeling that it was lonely in the garage, that it missed me, but I was the one who already missed everything. I don't mean Hopuonk itself, exactly, but more like the time when I was little, when Susan wanted to be around me and let me touch her hair, when I still wanted that too.

I switched on the transistor radio, which picked up a fuzzy signal of "Hunger Strike" by Temple of the Dog, which PJ sang an acoustic version of sometimes.

When I got to Corvis's house, I saw the lava lamp glowing in her bedroom window. I tossed the bike on her lawn. This act was one

I'd done hundreds of times as a kid, and it felt both strange and completely normal to do it now.

I pressed my face to the glass of her window and saw her curled in her desk chair, hugging her knees to her chest. I couldn't see her face, but she was bent over, writing something.

I rapped on the window.

Corvis turned to face me. Her face was splotchy and red, her eyes bloodshot. I'd gone there for some kind of comfort, and it had never occurred to me that Corvis might need that too.

I'd never seen Corvis cry before. Not when her grandmother died in fourth grade and they called her out of class. Not when she fell off her bike in fifth grade and plummeted into a ditch, breaking her arm. Not when everyone egged her house.

I waved, and she put her forefinger to her lips, quieting me. She stood and came to the window, yanking it open.

"What's up?" she said. She tried to pretend she hadn't been crying.

"Can I come in?" I asked.

"It's really late," she shout-whispered.

"Duh," I said.

Corvis sighed, then pulled the window open wider and helped me inside, holding me by the armpits. We both toppled onto the floor. This sneaking in through the window thing was much easier when we were eleven.

"What are you doing here?" she asked, picking herself up off the rug. In Corvis's house, they didn't have wall-to-wall—they had hundred-year-old Turkish rugs everywhere, in all shapes and sizes and color combinations.

I stayed on the floor.

"I couldn't sleep," I said. "Why were you crying?"

"I wasn't."

"Yes, you were."

I looked her up and down. She wore long pajamas and a red bathrobe. Her hair was, as always, a mess.

"What are you writing?" I tried, hoping for a different response.

"A letter," she said.

"To who?"

"Kristen, okay?" said Corvis. Fresh tears swelled in her eyes, and she clenched her jaw, trying to hold them in.

"It's okay," I said, looking at her. "You can cry."

She sat on the floor again, facing me.

"I broke up with her yesterday," said Corvis. "I decided to go to Sarah Lawrence early. You know, take a summer class. Get out of here."

"Okay," I said. A twinge went through my stomach, imagining Corvis somewhere else. Even though I was leaving, too, I still felt abandoned.

"She wanted to come, like I said, but that's a terrible idea. She needs to go be on her own, to find a boyfriend, to forget about me. But she begged me not to break up with her. She *begged* me. Then she turned our friends against me."

"I'm sorry," I said. It was difficult not to reach out and touch her, to comfort her.

Corvis shrugged and wiped her cheeks with the palm of her hand.

"This was always going to happen, but it still feels awful."

I thought of their friends—the kids from band, art class, and drama. They were either too skinny, too short, too fat, or too sweaty, wore ill-fitting dark clothing dotted with holes, and dyed their hair blue or purple. They pierced body parts that had no business being pierced. But they were just as petty, just as backstabbing as we were—and, just like us, they looked alike. They wore the same clothing. They left people out.

"You're going to Sarah Lawrence," I said. "You're going to meet people that are *so* much cooler than everyone here. It'll be okay."

"I know that," she said, "but it doesn't stop me from feeling bad."

"Everyone's against me too," I said. "Only they're pretending not to be just because my dad is Johnny Moon and he's coming here. I don't want to do this photo shoot. I don't think I want to be on the cover of a magazine."

"Why not?"

"People don't take him as seriously as he wants them to," I said. "Now they're making this into a big *reunion*, to help get him more publicity, and it feels like a scam."

Corvis nodded.

"Yeah," she said. "Fuck that."

"But I have to do it," I said. "I just wanted . . ."

"A dad?"

I took a deep breath.

"Yeah," I said.

"You don't have to do it," she said.

We sat in silence on the rug for a few minutes. It didn't feel right to touch her, even though she was still crying a little. I didn't think I had that privilege. Then I thought of something.

"Listen," I said. "We're both about to leave, and it's almost my birthday, and we're both feeling like shit. Let's do something crazy—let's go have an adventure."

"What do you have in mind?"

"Scottie's car," I said. "Let's go mess it up."

Corvis narrowed her eyes.

"Nothing permanent," she said. "No keying . . . nothing that will actually do damage, okay?"

"I pinky-promise," I said, holding out my pinky finger.

She linked her pinky in mine and shook.

"Got any Oreos?" I asked.

Corvis smiled.

———

We walked through the dark streets, plastic shopping bags of Double Stuf Oreos in our arms.

Scottie's truck was parked by The Mooring, where everyone would see it in the morning.

Corvis wasn't crying anymore. Her face was still blotchy, but she was suppressing laughter. In her pajamas, with her messy hair, she looked young.

"Okay," I said, pointing to Scottie's truck. "Spotted."

Corvis shot me a look.

"Ready?" I asked.

"Ready."

We dug into the Oreos, ripping the packages open with our teeth like dogs. One by one, we pulled the cookies apart and stuck them, frosting side down, to his windshield. The whole time, we laughed, and everything felt electric, and it felt like we were outlaws.

"Save the other halves," Corvis said.

We kept going until the glass surfaces on his truck were completely covered. It was balmy outside, and the cookies stuck easily.

By the end, we had a whole shopping bag full of other halves.

"These are going to be *such* a pain in the ass to get off," Corvis said.

"Scottie's so dumb he'll probably turn on the windshield wipers and break them," I said.

We sat on the ground, surveying the damage. It looked great. And once the sun came up, which would be pretty soon, the frosting would stick even better.

We lit cigarettes, looked out over the water, and ate the other halves of the cookies between drags. It was a good combination, even though without the frosting it was more noticeable that Oreos taste like cardboard.

"Corvis?" I asked. "What were you writing in that letter?"

Corvis sighed and ate another other half.

"Nothing. I don't know," she said.

"It's okay," I said. "I won't tell anyone."

"I guess I was trying to explain to Kristen why I broke up with her, but I've already said it all to her face, and it didn't get me anywhere. I thought if I wrote a letter, she'd have to hear me out. She couldn't interrupt me."

"You can't make people listen," I said, surprising myself. Talking to Susan, especially this year, had begun feeling like I was talking to a brick wall—no matter what I said, she heard what she wanted to hear. "It's not your fault."

"I know it's not my fault." Corvis looked close to tears again, but she swallowed and regained the expression of determination. This was something I'd seen Heather do many times, and it occurred to me that Corvis and Heather had a lot in common, that they actually would have been friends if they'd been allowed. If they would have allowed themselves.

"So," Corvis said in a small voice, "it's *not* my fault?"

I reached for her hand and squeezed it. She squeezed back.

Corvis McClellan was my best friend.

"It's not your fault," I said again. "You're one of the good ones."

———————

Veronica Michaels called later that morning, with even more suggestions about how my life should go.

If the photo shoot went well, Johnny Moon and his publicist wanted me to play the hot girl who dies first in a horror movie called *At Dawn They Bite*. If *that* went well, they wanted me to play the hot but spoiled older sister in a TV series calling *Homecoming*, about a family where the mom, who was married to this fancy criminal defense lawyer in San Francisco, gets a divorce and moves back to her hometown in Wyoming. They would shoot the pilot in Vancouver, starting in August.

He also gave me his cell phone number. He had a *cell phone*.

I thought of what Brad said, about everything already being decided for us. As it turned out, he was partially right in my case, though the outcome wasn't what I'd dreamed of. I was both the center of attention and an object, something to be fixed up and moved around. Like a cake topper you throw away after the wedding. Like a token.

Now that I had a new father, I also had a new name: Taylor Garland Moon.

"We just can't wait to see the splash you make," Veronica

continued. "You can come out here this summer, and we'll get everything started. Once the *Vanity Fair* issue hits the stands, people will know your face."

So before even meeting me, Johnny Moon had already decided I could go to California and be with him. I'd wanted to win him over with my personality, but once again, my face was the important thing.

"Stop," I said to Veronica, shooing Sandra out of the kitchen with my hand. "I'm not doing this."

"What do you mean, you're not doing this?" Veronica asked, her voice changing. She always sounded both cheerful and mechanical, but for once she sounded kind of human.

"This isn't what I signed up for," I said.

My insides were exploding—I couldn't believe I was turning this down, especially since I had no idea how else to leave Hopuonk. Still, I just couldn't do it.

"This is what it feels like, all the time," I said. "Everyone watching me, everyone expecting something, but at least here it's just one town. I'm not about to let the whole world see me that way. Plus, I haven't even met him yet. I haven't even *talked* to him. Why hasn't he called me?"

"I don't understand." Veronica's voice sounded panicked now. She didn't answer my last question. Instead, she said, "This is every girl's dream."

"I want to meet him," I said. "Just not like this."

"I don't understand," she repeated.

"I'll keep the name," I said, "but cancel the photo shoot, and everything else."

After I hung up, I dodged Sandra in the hallway and shut myself inside my bedroom. I knew Sandra would be disappointed that I wasn't going to be on the cover of a magazine, and I didn't know what else I would do with my life, but I took the plane ticket out of my purse and ripped it into shreds over my trash can.

Wherever I was going, I needed to do it on my own.

The Pinecone

While I sat there in my folding chair at graduation, I thought about Sandra, and what she must have felt in one of these same chairs, back in 1979. It was May 30th, 2000, a date that had been unimaginable to me not long ago.

My cap kept slipping down my forehead while PJ sang "Fields of Gold," the graduation song. The valedictorian, some tech kid named Matt McDonald, who I'd never spoken to, gave a speech about friendship and knowledge, which made my hands sweat. Friendship and knowledge were so big, like impenetrable stone walls.

The "diploma" Principal Deftose gave me at the ceremony would be an empty sheet of paper. The administration decided I could walk at graduation, but that I needed to complete summer school in algebra and biology to earn my actual diploma. The sheet of paper was symbolic, meant to save me from embarrassment, but also to keep me in Hopuonk a little bit longer.

But I wasn't embarrassed. I was kind of proud, to be honest. My other secret was this: I threw the packet from Massachusetts College of Pharmacy and Health Sciences in the trash that morning without checking if I'd been accepted. Sandra, and everyone else, should have known better. I barely remembered to floss my own teeth. I didn't care if I graduated from high school. I thought it was kind of funny that they couldn't claim their shining star as an actual graduate.

Kristen Duffy was sitting almost directly in front of me at the ceremony. There was an entire pinecone stuck in her hair. I reached out to remove it, and as soon as I touched her, she spun around.

"How can you not notice that there's a pinecone in your hair?" I said angrily. I snatched it and handed it to her.

She took it, and instead of throwing it on the grass, she put it in her pocket.

"It's things like that, you know," I said. "Keeping pinecones that came out of your hair. Wearing safety pins as earrings. That's why everyone thinks you're weird."

Kristen looked like she was about to cry—her chin crinkled up like a walnut.

"That," I said, "and the fact that you wear pit-bull collars as jewelry."

"Why are you such a bitch?" she whispered.

"You better leave Corvis alone," I said. Then I dismissed Kristen forever.

Corvis spoke as salutatorian, and I couldn't get myself to pay attention to her actual words, except the end. I just watched her mouth moving, and though I wanted to, I didn't cry.

"Synonyms for the word 'commencement,'" I heard Corvis say, "are 'beginning,' 'dawn,' 'threshold.' I wish you all, all of my classmates, a good morning. And while you're out in the world after high school, I hope you all remember where you came from."

She was talking to herself, really. Most of the kids sitting in front of her were not leaving Hopuonk. But Corvis was afraid of forgetting, and so was I.

While I listened to Corvis's voice, I realized LA wasn't for me anyway. I decided I would try to get to San Francisco instead: Where D.J. and Stephanie Tanner lived. Where there were mountains and gay people. Where there were coffee shops everywhere. I knew how to make coffee.

The Last Check

L ater that night, I realized that I didn't own a suitcase. Of course I didn't—why would I? In my imagination, I saw myself packing a leather suitcase full of not clothes but trinkets—turkey feathers, seashells, shards of sea glass, even sand—and maybe some jewels that had been in my family for generations, though we had none of those either.

In reality, I packed the overnight bag with a few pairs of underwear and Stinky Lewis's dog food, examined it, and decided it looked neither beautiful nor useful, and left it behind. At the last moment, in the darkness, with the sound of the waves lapping the shore of Humming Rock Beach outside my window, I decided that I would figure out what I needed while I was moving.

I did, for some reason, grab the prom crown and put it on, and Stinky Lewis followed me. I brought only the chocolate box of cash and his food. Then, at the last minute, I grabbed the German sex toy that Corvis bought me in Provincetown.

I tiptoed into Sandra's room, where she slept curled on her side. The sun was just rising, and a slant of pale yellow hit her cheek.

I walked over to her bedside, lifted the hair from her face, and leaned down to kiss her cheek.

"I have to go," I whispered. She was angry with me for skipping out on the photo shoot, and she planned to let me live with her only while I finished summer school. I didn't tell her about my plan to leave, or that I wasn't visiting Johnny Moon. I didn't want her to try and stop me, so I figured I would find a pay phone somewhere along the way, maybe in Arizona or some other unimaginable place, and tell her then.

I hadn't told anyone but Stinky Lewis.

Sandra stirred but didn't wake up. Tears burned my eyes, because she was so beautiful that it was sad, because she looked small and young, because I didn't know whether she needed me.

"I love you," I whispered, running my forefinger down her arm. I saw, on her cheek, the shadow of my prom crown.

"I love you too, honey," she whispered back, still asleep, and rolled over.

I would stop at Emmylou's for my last check, and then I would drive away.

———

I got to Emmylou's just as it opened.

Heather stood behind the counter, her eyes red, arranging the pastries. Just before graduation, her father moved into a house on the beach and bought himself a small airplane. Today, I noticed a stain on her Emmylou's shirt, something she usually never would have let happen.

The sun hadn't finished rising, and I'd always thought the darkness outside gave the bright lights and color scheme of Emmylou's a sinister feel. Now, looking around for the last time, my heart pulled slightly at my chest. I didn't realize how great my love was for the small pockets of Hopuonk that I felt belonged to me, and I was beginning to understand that the feeling of homesickness would hit me later, in moments when I didn't expect it.

"I'm leaving today," I said to Heather. "I came to say goodbye."

As those words left my lips, I realized that they weren't true.

Holding out a plastic-wrapped cinnamon bun, Heather said, "For the plane."

"I'm not flying," I said. "I'm not going to LA."

My Volvo was parked out front, and Stinky Lewis sat shotgun, ears up, waiting for me to come back. We stood staring at each other, and then "As I Lay Me Down" came on the radio *again*.

"What do you mean?" she asked. "Where are you going?"

The cinnamon bun hung between us. I leaned over the counter, put my hand on her wrist, and gripped her tight.

"I was thinking San Francisco," I said. She didn't move her wrist, so I held it tighter. Her personality was so big that it was easy to forget how thin she was, how fragile.

She looked at me, sighed, and said, "We all have herpes, you know."

"What?"

She put down the cinnamon bun.

"Think about it," she said. "We've all been with each other. We share diseases, along with everything else."

I walked around to the other side of the counter, my last check forgotten by then, and took her hands in mine. She squirmed just a little, but then stopped and looked back at me. She wasn't wearing any makeup, and her cheeks were flushed, her eyelashes so blond they were nearly white. It had been a really long time since I saw her without makeup on.

"I know it might not work," I said. "And there's a real possibility everything will get fucked-up, but you're coming with me. Don't you want to try and do something different with your life? You know, do makeup for real?"

She stared at me, and her eyebrows furrowed.

And then, in a smaller voice, I asked, "Don't you want me?"

Tears formed in her eyes, and they looked like they were made of glass.

"Of course I do," she said.

I put my hand flat on the small of her back, and pulled her toward me.

"Come with me," I whispered into her mouth.

"Now?"

I pulled out the chocolate box, quickly showing her the money.

"Yes," I said. "People do this, you know. People run away. People start over."

Stinky Lewis barked once and let out a long whine.

"Before it gets light outside," I said.

She leaned into me, and for the first time since New Year's Eve, she wrapped both arms around me.

"I always forget how small you are," she said.

"So do I," I said.

I hoisted myself onto the counter and took her face in my hands. Somehow, though I'd never felt this way before, I knew how to kiss her. One hand on the back of her neck, one hand on her back. I thought I'd known with Susan, but this was different.

She knew too. I felt her fingers in my hair, my crown dropping to the floor.

I tasted her salty tears, and I understood that they were tears of relief, and also of fear. I shared those feelings.

She pulled away just for a second and said, "I can't promise that I won't hurt you, but I can promise that I'll try not to."

"So that's a yes?"

She fell into me, her weight against me, her face buried in my neck. "This is so crazy," she whispered.

I wrapped my legs around her waist and held her.

"Let's go be crazy," I whispered.

"Okay," Heather said, untying her apron and tossing it aside. "Fuck it."

It felt a little bit like jumping off Fourth Cliff, only *more*. I took her hand again and led her outside with me, our hips bumping together. Heather laughed, tossing the keys aside without even locking up.

As we climbed into the car—me in my prom crown and Heather in her Emmylou's uniform—I realized that I had no idea where I'd be on my eighteenth birthday but that I wanted Heather with me.

"I've always loved you," she said from the passenger seat. This time, she looked straight at me.

"Me too," I said, touching her cheek. "Cliff jumpers for life." Then I kissed her again before I turned the key in the ignition and sped onto the highway, away from the sand-covered roads.

Soon, in Hopuonk, summer would be in full swing. After that, the fall would come, and the leaves would start turning. Then the leaf peepers would come down from Boston to see the foliage, with their collars popped and their belts tight. Once they were satisfied, they would turn and go right back to their fancy little brownstones in the city.

Then the leaves would die and fall and snow would cover them up, just like they were never there at all.

Acknowledgments

Huge thanks to my editor, Arianne Lewin, and my agent, Nathaniel Jacks.

Thank you, also, to *Epoch Magazine* at Cornell University for publishing the opening chapter as a short story.

The MacDowell Colony and Virginia Center for the Creative Arts provided me with much-needed time and space to work on this book, as well as a community of artists who continue to inspire me. Special thanks to my residency bestie, Kamala Nair—I couldn't have done this without your feedback and friendship.

I'm eternally grateful to my students and colleagues at Loyola New Orleans and the faculty at Beloit College, Columbia University, and Florida State University. And to Dick Gardner from Marshfield High School—even though I only got a B- in AP English, you showed me that I wasn't the moron I thought I was.

To all of my friends, both inside and outside the writing community, especially those of you who looked at drafts of this book, I love you beyond earthly description. Special thanks to Lexy Olsen for a lifetime of stories and fake vampires.

To my family, especially my cousins, Jebb and Jules, and my brilliant Mum who raised me by herself, you are wicked sad.

And to Julie Buck, you are the most wonderful and supportive partner I could ever ask for. But scissoring still isn't a thing.